MY
PUCKING
MATES

ISBN (E-Book): 978-1-964220-14-7
ISBN (Paperback Ingram Spark): 978-1-964220-15-4
ISBN (Hardback Ingram Spark): 978-1-964220-16-1

Edited by Jaquelyn Vale, She Who Edits LLC
Paperback Front Cover Design by Izzy Elliott (cartoons by @ArtByToniii)
Formatting, Paperback Wrap & Hardcover Design by Aurelia Dunbar of Mayonaka Designs

Published by Izzy Elliott LLC

To every little girl or boy that had to grow up too early and never really got to be taken care of. It's okay to let people in. It's okay to let someone take care of you.

Also, to all my readers that have been asking for the twin's mate since book 1. I hope it's everything you dreamed it would be.

before you continue!

My Pucking Mates is the fourth book in the Pucking Werewolves series and is an IMMEDIATE continuation of My Pucking Life and contains graphic sexual scenes involving three people with DP.

My Pucking Mate should be read first, as this is an ongoing storyline and not interconnected standalones.

This installment of the series will not progress the core plot of the main series that you've read so far. This book is about the communication and connection between Eris, Dolos, and Runa.

The main story will resume in the fifth installment.

A complete list of the series tropes and triggers can be found at IzzyElliott.com

1
ERIS

10 Years Old

Being quiet is so hard for Dolos. It's my job to help him stay silent while we sit on the edge of the vast fields ahead of us. I finally convinced Pop to teach us how to hunt. He doesn't think we're ready. I heard him tell Mama we're still too immature.

But I want to prove him wrong. I want to show him that we can do this. We can learn. We can help provide for Mama and the family.

The problem is that we've already been out here for hours, and nothing has happened. Dolos is getting twitchy. He can't physically sit still this long. He's not trying to misbehave or disrespect Pop; he's just wired different.

I hate the look my twin brother gets on his face when he gets in trouble just for being who he is. He's not a bad boy like Pop says he is. He's happy and kind and helpful. It's not his fault he has trouble staying focused and sitting still. He's not a bad boy…but sometimes, he can be too much for people who don't understand him.

I've started working on mimicking some of the things he does so that he doesn't feel so alone for just being himself...but only when Pop isn't around.

He's my twin brother. We're supposed to be the same person. We look the same if you put us in front of a looking glass, but whatever we're made up of on the inside is just different.

I'd rather sit and read, enjoying the peace. Learn to hunt and fish. Help with work and chores. While he can't seem to focus on tasks and directions long enough to enjoy what he's doing.

"Dammit, Eris!" Pop roars, interrupting my thoughts.

I was only distracted for a minute before my head snaps toward the sound of our father's angry voice, finding my brother's feet barely touching the ground. Pop's giant scarred fist is bunched in Dolos' shirt, their noses nearly touching. Pop growls as Dolos pinches his eyes shut tight, his shoulders nearly touching his ears, trying to curl in on himself.

I scramble across the small space between us, immediately trying to wedge myself between them.

He tosses Dolos to the ground and snatches me up, but I don't lock up like my little brother does.

"Thought you wanted to learn? Thought you were gonna keep him quiet?" he barks at me, but I refuse to cower, only responding, "Yes, sir."

His eyes narrow, that big, blue vein in his forehead throbbing as he gets more and more upset that I'm not afraid of him like Mama and Dolos are.

Someday, he'll be afraid of me. Someday, he'll regret the way he's treated us. Someday, Mama and Dolos won't have to deal with his temper…ever again.

2
ERIS

Present

Even if I'd been able to lately, there would be no sleeping in today. The townhouse is thrumming with energy from the traveling party, as well as those of us being left behind.

I'm trying really fucking hard not to be bitter about it and let my attitude get me into any more shit with Roman, but I'm stuck between a rock and a hard place here. The only one that understands is Dolos, and even he doesn't fully understand…no one does.

Staring at my ceiling from where I lay on my fully made bed, I consider whether or not to get up and spend time with my pack before some of them leave for a week.

I know they'll be safe, but as Roman pointed out, this will be the first time he's gone on a mission of any kind without me and my brother… because of me.

I know that he's upset with me, but my Alpha and Luna are still two of the most important people in my existence—along with Benny, I suppose…and Andrei too.

Fuck! Why does it have to be like this? Dolos and I were doing just fine without a mate. What's considered a blessing to so many is something that causes a state of constant panic and near-terror within me.

He must have felt my uncertainty because he's got his joker face on as he barrels into my bedroom without a care in the world.

My twin and I have a much closer bond than that of regular siblings, families, or pack members. I can't compare it to a mate bond, having never experienced that kind of connection, which leaves me to assume it's similar. He is sometimes even able to realize something is wrong with me before I can realize it myself.

"Come on, grumpapotamus! Time to go play nice with the others before they leave," Dolos sing-songs dramatically with his arms spread wide, filling the space with his lighter energy.

Now that the world has seen my true disposition, it's been so much harder to tuck it back into the crevices of my being. For so much of my existence, I've spent all my time around others, matching Dolos' energy.

While there's no way he fully understands, it's almost as though he's somehow always known. He's not having trouble acclimating to my change in demeanor. If anything, he's rolled into his goofiness even harder, like he's compensating for the lack of mine.

"I haven't decided if I'm coming out yet."

He scoffs and smiles, moving around my bed and plopping onto the mattress beside me. He wiggles for a minute, getting comfortable, before he stills, his hands resting behind his head to match mine.

"What do you need?" he asks quietly, more seriously.

Without a clear answer to his question, I heave a heavy sigh that does nothing to release the pressure of the boulder pressing down on my chest.

"There has to be something I can do to help," he begs me to give him something, but there's truly nothing he can do. I don't know how to consider the possibility of the future they both deserve.

Deciding that being uncomfortable in front of everyone would be better than staying here while my twin flays me open with his concern, I push myself off the bed, stretching slowly as I rise. He leaps off the bed, his smile firmly back in place, rubbing his hands together in excitement.

"Don't push it. Let me work through this as best I can." It was supposed to be a request, but it came out as more of a bark.

Of course, he doesn't take it seriously. He's laughing and opening the door, waiting for me to walk into the hallway ahead of him.

As per the new usual, when we enter the space, all conversation and movement stop. All eyes on us. Including hers. The greenest fucking eyes I've ever seen. If we hadn't already found the lost princess, I would have suggested it could be her.

When our eyes lock, my entire body turns to stone, and I can't move. I've been more careful to not have these moments. They're debilitating. The pull of our bond becomes stronger and more painful every moment I keep myself from her.

It makes me feel like such a fucking ass to be putting her and my brother through the same experience. It doesn't help to know that if I weren't part of the equation, they would have already completed their mate bond—and be happy—like they both deserve. Dolos would have dove in headfirst, as he so often does with all things in his life.

Hanging my head, I move around the space to the corner of the room. From here, I'm out of everyone's way, but I can still keep my eyes on my family. *FUCK. Why can't I just get the fuck over all of the shit that plagues me from the past? How does Leera roll with the punches like she does?* With everything that's been thrown at her, she still beams. Sunshine and happiness surround her, and I envy her ability to pack the shit away and focus on the good things in life.

The result of my wandering thoughts has now caused me to be off my guard and unprepared for her approach. *Why do her eyes have to be so green and…fucking perfect?* I sigh to myself, but she notices and wrinkles her forehead like she's trying to understand me.

"You can't avoid me forever," she whispers in a pained voice, for only me to hear. Without waiting for my response or reaction, she marches right past me, wiggling herself between Roman and Leera to wrap an arm around each of them and squeezing them tightly together.

I don't know if it's her words, her actions, or my need to physically touch her that is causing a fist to clench around my heart, making it hard to breathe beneath the pressure.

With his always optimal timing, Dolos settles beside me, bumping me with his shoulder as he does. I'm rubbing the sore place in my chest, willing it all away. He notices the gesture and grunts, "It's not just you hurting, you know?" His signature smile is gone again—because of me—and he also rubs at the same spot on his chest. "This affects all three of us. Please…tell me what you need," he begs again, but I don't know how to tell him that I don't know if I'm capable of loving her the way she deserves. Fuck, I don't know if I'm capable of loving anything…"

With the words locked inside of me, I nudge him back in what I hope comes across as playful and try to smile, but the once-constant expression now feels foreign on my face as I turn to rummage through the fridge. I don't even know what I'm looking for, but I quickly grab a bottle of electrolytes when the fridge beeps at me for having the door open too long, garnering a few glances from the group.

I loathe the way everyone looks at me right now, like a grenade that's pin has been pulled and everyone's just waiting for it to go off. I could probably even get over the looks if I didn't know what the looks mean. But I do. I know it's a mixture of pity and pissed off because I'm being an asshole to my mate and twin. I'm losing the trust and confidence of the only people that have ever cared about us.

FUCK.

Roman and Leera make their way around the room—Leera hugging everyone while Roman continues watching her every move, following whatever she says with his usual grunt or nod. I wasn't expecting the slightly suffocating hug she granted me, holding on what seemed like longer than she hugged some of the others. What I was expecting even less was for her to lock her icy-blue eyes on mine and use the pack link to tell me that she expects progress by the time they return. It wasn't a threat…exactly…but the look in her eyes and the shiver that rolled through me told me that's exactly what it was. She may be small, but the energy she exudes is not. Paired with that of our Alpha, the worlds had better watch out.

I do the only thing I can do right now—I offer her a small nod to let her know that I'll do my best.

While they'll feel as though they've been gone for three weeks, it will only be a week here. The thought that we could get that much—if anything—accomplished in a single week…well, I have to try something, or I have a feeling I'll be in the doghouse…and I'm not certain it would be a metaphorical one.

The second the door closes behind the travel party, I allow my squared shoulders to drop. I turn on my heel, planning to make a beeline for the gym, but Khaos blocks my path with his arms crossed and left eyebrow raised.

Releasing a heavy sigh, I pick my shoulders back up, cross my arms, and set my feet shoulder-width apart. "You going to start in on me now, too? They just fucking left," I snap at him.

The right side of his lips twitches as though he's fighting a grin. "Not exactly," he states firmly, but I can practically see the thoughts tumbling around in his head, looking for the right way to handle the situation. His shoulders drop a fraction. *Why does he look defeated?*

"Look…I know me being part of the group is new enough, and I'm not about to act like I know what you're going through—"

"I feel like there's a 'but' coming," I snap at him in the middle of his monologue.

The genuine smile that stretches across his face is a little unsettling as he continues, "There is. I just wanted to remind you that we've all been through some serious shit. There's not one person here that's had a merry-little-life full of sunshine and rainbows."

I open my mouth to smart-off again, but he notices and raises his hand, his smiling eyes now glaring at me—effectively shutting me up.

"The point is that we all have baggage. Everyone fucking does. All species of creatures. It's time for you to man up and talk shit out. She's all I have left of my pack, and I won't watch her in pain...*unnecessary* pain, for very much longer."

He pauses, allowing me to speak, but I don't. What could I even say? He's not wrong. Knowing what each of my packmates has been through… It feels even more selfish to be feeling this way…But how do I move past this?

"Anyways…Slate and I will be going to the pack to make introductions and see if they need anything. Miss Tilly will be joining us." He stares at me, waiting for me to acknowledge his implication. "Talk to her. Or them. Whatever you need to do. You have to let the demons out…or let her move on. But you have a choice to make."

3
DOLOS

12 Years Old

I wake, startled as I jolt and crack my forehead on Eris' top bunk. Groaning and rubbing my forehead, I try to unscramble my brain to figure out what woke me. That's when I hear it. Mama is yelling, and it sounds like things are being broken.

Something shatters against a wall, and I leap out of bed, but I'm not the only one awake now. Eris launches himself from his bunk and lands ahead of me as we move towards the door. He turns towards me with a serious look I've never seen on his face, but I'm struck with a déjà vu kind of feeling…like I vaguely remember he used to be more like that.

Shaking the foggy memories from my mind, I worry about what's got Mama so upset. Did I do something to upset him again?

We've gotten better at avoiding Pop and his foul moods—mostly by just making ourselves scarce. It's easier to goof off and enjoy ourselves away from his disapproving glare. I never even understood why he was so angry all the time. I swear, there's nothing that anyone could do to make that monster happy.

Even when we're on our best behavior, he complains. When Mama cooks the best meals, he complains. If we all head into town for something, he complains. I can't remember a time that I've ever seen him happy.

Eris snaps his fingers just in front of my nose, bringing me back to the moment, eyes taking a lethal edge.

He leans his head around the door frame, scoping out what's going on before he waves his hand for me to follow him. He flattens his palm and moves it as though he's pressing down on something, wordlessly instructing me to lower myself.

We slowly, and as quietly as we can, move down the hall towards where we heard a commotion.

Eris turns the corner first, and his entire frame locks still. Moving closer to see what's going on, I squeeze myself between him and the doorframe, unprepared for the sight before me.

Mama is lying in the middle of the kitchen floor, curled up in the fetal position. I don't see any blood or signs of physical harm, but there are shattered dishes and debris on the floor around her as she sobs, clutching her chest.

On reflex, I rush in and drop onto my knees beside her, scanning her body, making sure she's not injured. "Mama, what's wrong? What happened? Are you okay?" I plead, gently moving her hair from her face.

I don't like her face when she cries. She has the sweetest face when she's calm and peaceful. We don't get to see it enough because of Pop, but those moments are precious.

Her gray eyes that look just like mine and Eris' look back at me, full of angry red veins, swollen, and still glistening with tears. "I'm so sorry… my sweet boys," is all she says before she closes her eyes, and her muscles all relax.

"Mama!" I shout, my head whipping back to where Eris still stands locked in place.

"Do something!" I yell, throwing a larger shard of what might have been a plate at him.

It works, and he stumbles towards where I'm crouched over Mama, and the deadly look on his face would be terrifying if he wasn't my brother.

He checks her pulse and says it's erratic but strong as he looks her over for visible injuries. Finding none, he moves around the space looking for signs of what in the world happened here while I remain at Mama's side, holding her hand in mine, rubbing circles on her skin like she did on mine when I was younger.

I'm nudged awake and confused before the middle-of-the-night's events replay in my mind. The sun hasn't fully risen yet, but I'm lying in the middle of a now clean kitchen floor with a still-sleeping Mama. Eris looks like he never went back to sleep; he must have cleaned the kitchen.

"Where's Pop? Does he know what happened to Mama?" I ask, keeping my voice low, trying not to wake her.

His mouth sets in a thin line. "He left."

I'm still tired, and it takes a few moments for the words to register. "Wait…What do you mean he left?"

His fists clench at his sides, and he looks like he's having a mental argument with himself. "He left Dolos. He rejected her. He severed their mate bond. And he left. End of story."

My eyes feel like they're about to bug out of my head. *Is it my fault? I know Pop and I didn't get along, but I would never want Mama to have to go through the pain of losing her mate.* That's one of the worst things a werewolf can go through. "W-why?" is all I can say, the words nearly getting stuck in my throat.

"Because he's a piece of shit!" Eris barks, using a bad word because Mama's still asleep and can't hear to scold him. "He never treated her right. He never treated you right. He never treated any of us right. Some mate.

Some father. Some man." He angrily spits the words, crosses his arms over his chest, and takes in the space.

I notice he's not wearing his sleep clothes he had on when we woke the first time. "Why are you already dressed?"

A flicker of something flits across his face so fast I'm pretty sure I must have imagined it. "The sun's coming up. I got ready for the day. It's our job to take care of Mama now." With his short, sharp words, he moves towards us, crouching low and cradling her in his arms. He rises steadily, carrying her down the hall to her bed. After he lays her gently, he tucks her in and leaves a light kiss on her forehead. His face is void of emotion as he walks back out of the room…like it doesn't even bother him that Pop is gone.

4
DOLOS

Present

I lift my head from the back of the couch where I was resting it and maybe eavesdropping a little on Khaos and Eris. We…I mean, I…may be a goof, but that's far from all I am. Eris and I are Roman's spies for a reason. When he needs someone to slink around, get answers, and follow people, that's our job.

I had to learn to control my energy and distractions at a young age, or everyone in our home would pay for it. Mama got the worst of it, but Eris would always step in to save both Mama and me from Pop's wrath. I wish I could have been a stronger kid, but once we grew into the men we are, I was determined to never feel that way again.

I hadn't thought about that night in ages…

Mama ended up sleeping for four days before she finally woke up, sad and weak. By the time she came to, Eris had returned to his jovial self, seeming to match my happiness and energy as usual. It made me wonder if I had imagined the events of that night.

I feel like I've always known that the way twelve-year-old Eris acted that night was who he really was. I vaguely remembered him being that way when we were much younger, but again, I left it in my imagination.

With everything that's happened recently, it's clear my intuition was right this whole time. I just don't understand why. Why would he put on a show for everyone? Why would he put on a show for me? There were so many things I needed answers to, but my questions would have to wait.

The most important thing was getting through to Eris enough for him to see what's right in fucking front of us. Our mate.

Does sharing our mate make things different?

In some ways, yes, but not the ones you'd think. We often shared our women anyways. We're identical twins that play hockey. If a woman—or puck bunny—likes one of us, she will usually like the other.

But with a mate, things will be so much different.

We never had a "relationship" last longer than a month. People get tired of our liveliness and antics easily. The men—and now, women—who live in this house are the only beings that have ever truly cared for us—other than Mama, of course.

Not only are we fully unprepared for a solid relationship, but sharing a mate means we must be on the same page. I've been ready to complete the bond since the second her scared, bright green eyes met mine. When her eyes didn't stay on mine and instead bounced between mine and Eris'…I knew…and it just made sense to me. I found myself feeling…relieved.

Why would the Goddess grant us different mates that could pull us apart when she could provide us with a mate to share?

What I didn't expect was Eris' total shift in…well, existence. We've been the wild, crazy, fun twins for centuries.

Is this new Eris the real one? Why has he been…pretending for so long?

Shaking away all the thoughts clouding my brain, I hop off the couch and head for my twin.

When I reach him, I wrap my arm around his shoulder and pull him towards his room. "I don't—"

"Oh, trust me, I know. You don't want to do anything, and you most certainly don't want to talk about it...but it's time, big brother." I put the silliness away and let the feelings coursing through me show on my face as I shut his door. "I deserve to know what's going on in that big brain of yours. *We* deserve to know what's going on and what comes next," I say, slumping onto the trunk at the end of his bed.

He begins pacing the space in front of me, running his hands through his hair.

I try to stay patient, I do, but after...I don't know how many minutes, I can't help myself. "Look, I know we did some shit for the armies. I know we indulged in our fair share of women. And I know we're not the easiest people to deal with...but I don't know what any of that has to do with not accepting our mate, Eris..."

He stops and stares at me long enough that I think he won't speak. I'm having to learn my brother all over again, and I fucking hate it. I can see for certain in his eyes that *this* is the man that's been beneath his skin the whole time. *This* is my brother. While I don't yet understand why...it also settles something within me. Maybe my wolf? Shit, I don't know anymore.

His mouth opens and closes a few times like he's trying to decide how to communicate what he needs to say and stills when he settles on, "Do you remember the night Pop left?"

I jerk slightly where I sit, having just thought about that night. Without knowing what to say, I nod while he paces.

"He was her fated mate," he begins, his voice laced with frustration and anger. "He was mean to her. He was mean to you. What kind of fated mate treats his life partner and children like that?" His voice begins to rise as though these feelings have been simmering since that night and are now boiling over. "She deserved to be happy. You deserved to be yourself!"

He stops and stares at me and...what the fuck am I supposed to say? All I can do is watch him unravel.

"I didn't have a choice! He hurt her again, and it had to be the last time! I wouldn't let him hurt either of you ever a-fucking-gain!" He shakes his head, both hands in his hair, and when he raises his face back to mine, his eyes are red and full of tears I've never seen in my brother's eyes.

Rising from the trunk, I intend to move towards him, but he backs away from me just as the door bursts open.

5 Runa

Khaos, Slate, and Miss Tilly—being the meddlesome bunch they are—decided it was best they go to the pack for a few days to see if we could work anything out. *We* being Eris, Dolos, and myself. *Anything* being deciding what we do about our mate bond.

I've been sitting on the couch since they left, fiddling with a blanket, while I try to think of how I can get them to communicate with me...At least let me know what's going on. I've spent my entire life having to be strong all the time, and I'm so tired. I just want to *be*.

Earlier, I noticed Dolos dragging Eris away from Khaos. I'm not sure what's going on, but their tempers are clouding the townhouse in tension.

I tried to wait on the couch for them to come through the space organically. I wanted to try and strike up a real conversation, but just sitting and waiting here is making me twitchy.

When their energies become so loud and…*pained*…I can't sit still any longer. My feet carry me to Eris' bedroom door. It's a space I know I'm not welcome, but I can't help the tension of his pain suffocating me, and not do *something*. The fact that it's this strong with our bond incomplete, makes my heart hurt for him.

Without contemplation or hesitation, I fling his bedroom door open. Their attention simultaneously snaps towards me. Eris' eyes are especially wild, and I can feel his wolf riding him hard. Dolos looks exasperated for his brother and whatever he's trying to discuss.

I bolt across the space and fling myself into Eris, wrapping my arms around him, latching on with all my might. There's an inkling of fear I don't want to give life to, that he'll shake me off.

He smells like bonfires and autumn nights. A sigh escapes me as I greedily inhale his scent.

Surprised he hasn't pulled away or pushed me off of him yet, I very slowly lift my chin enough to open one eye to check the status of my surroundings.

Seeing Dolos first, I find his jaw is practically on the floor.

I've never been able to get so close to him, and now that I'm here…I never want to leave. When I can't avoid it a second longer, I decide to chance a look at Eris. With my cheek still smashed against his chest, I tilt my head to sneak a peek up at him, taking in as much as I can. What I find isn't as bad as I was expecting, but it's not as good as my silly little heart had hoped. His head is tilted slightly away from me with his eyes clamped shut and jaw locked tight.

While he's tolerating my abrupt touch, not pulling away as I expected he would, I allow myself to melt into him. Testing my limits further, I turn and elongate my neck, the column of my throat now resting against his chest.

His heartbeat thrums through me as I unabashedly gaze at one of my mates. Staring straight at his face is kind of like trying to stare at the sun; he's so damn beautiful, it nearly hurts. His golden skin looks so soft aside from the angry, throbbing vein crawling up his neck. His strong jawline dusted with a day or two of growth, which might be the longest I've ever seen it. His annoyingly long eyelashes. His high cheekbones. The way I dream of running my hands through his ruffled blonde hair.

I wish I could see his gray eyes—the same gray as Dolos', but somehow, they're sharper, keeping everyone at arm's length.

Leera was telling me that he wasn't like this when she met them. She told me how they were the goofiest and orneriest people she'd ever met. *Did I do this to him?*

I could see those attributes in Dolos, but it seems impossible for this twin. He's been nothing but cold, distant, and daunting since the sight of him stole my breath.

The moment I realized they were both my mates was the strangest experience of my life. My wolf was whining and pawing to be released, wanting her mate. For the both of us—my wolf and I—to realize there were two of them was a shock.

Especially after losing our entire pack—apart from our Alpha. He later told me how he would have perished as well if it weren't for Leera. He went on to explain that she was his soul-sister, in a way, and everything that had transpired to date. I've since gotten Leera's side of the story as well, and it's something straight out of the legends we were told as pups.

Not only was she reincarnated by the Moon Goddess to return to her mate, Roman, and her brother, Khaos, in this lifetime, but she has also been gifted with several powers, some of which we have yet to understand. Her healing powers are what saved Khaos, without her even knowing what she was doing.

With the recent loss of our entire pack, there wasn't really time for introductions and mate bonds. The perished deserved our utmost attention and respect while being returned to the Goddess' embrace.

The movement of Eris' arms pulls me from my thoughts and back to the moment. I brace myself, and my heart, as I fully expect him to remove me from his personal space. Instead, Dolos and I gasp simultaneously when his arms lock around me.

Fuck, I didn't want to cry. I just wanted him to not be in so much pain.

Leera's hugs have shown me how important they are, and I just reacted. For him to return my embrace is like nothing I ever expected. His strong arms are holding me, and my body is going haywire, happily losing its shit. The mate bond tingling across my skin everywhere we meet, begging me to complete the bond, but that's not my choice. They have to want me.

I don't move. I barely even breathe. Terrified that I'll wake up and this will have all been some kind of dream, wild hallucination, or worse… That it's real, and he'll come to his senses and throw me out of his room and…reject me.

My wolf whimpers at the thought, and he must have picked up on it because his eyes flash open, and…I'm not prepared for what I see. There's a thunderstorm brewing in his dark gray eyes. There are shocks of silver and flecks of black among the storm clouds gathering in his irises.

He looks me over as though something was physically wrong with me, but still, I don't move. Too scared to even blink until my burning eyes force me to, needing the hydration.

I don't know how long we stand there in silence while a war wages within him. Dolos has slowly begun to approach us like you would a scared and wounded wild animal. When he reaches us and we're still locked in the embrace that I refuse to let go of first, he moves to stand right next to us.

Not behind me and joining the hug in a way that would sandwich me between them—*wouldn't that be amazing?*—but instead, he's at my right side, Eris' left, where I continue to refuse to let go of this hug.

Leera once told me, "You should never be the first to let go of a hug, because you never know just how badly the other person might need it."

I think she's on to something, because if anyone needs a hug this long, it's apparently Eris.

Still moving at the speed of a hundred-year-old tortoise, Dolos lifts his left hand, placing it on the small of my back, and it takes all my self-control not to moan at the contact. With both of them touching me, all my nerve endings are being fried, and tingles are shooting through my bloodstream.

I'm clearly not the only one affected as his eyes close and his head falls back. When he returns his head to the upright position, he clasps his brother on the shoulder with a look of adoration on his face.

I don't know yet what these men have been through, but I know it's a lot, and they love each other even more for it.

Dolos moves closer to us, and like everything else I've noticed about them, they are polar opposites—he smells like blooming trees and spring rain.

My body is full of so many feelings. The most overwhelming sensation is blinding happiness. I scold myself for being weak when a single tear escapes and rolls down my cheek, but it doesn't fall because Dolos catches it with his finger and makes a show of putting it in the square breast pocket of his T-shirt.

I turn my head towards him, resting my ear on Eris' chest, listening to the thrashing of his heart for as long as I can…in case this is the only time I'm ever allowed to hear it.

Dolos is watching me, and his eyes are a much lighter gray today. I've noticed from a distance that both of their eyes' colors seem to change with the weather, what they're wearing, and their moods.

Today his eyes are a brighter gray with an almost navy-looking ring around them.

Goddess, they're so beautiful.

"Runa," Eris says, and my heart rate spikes, my legs going weak. That's the first time he's ever said my name.

Please don't be the last, I beg the Goddess and whatever deities will listen.

Dolos' hand on my back tenses as we wait for his twin's words.

"Thank you."

Two words from him shouldn't do what they do to me. I turn my eyes back to his and swear, "Always."

I shouldn't have said that, but I can't take it back now…but it's true, nonetheless. "Can we try to…talk?" I whisper.

He closes his eyes, but when he opens them, they look like the calm after the storm. "Can Dolos and I have a moment to finish the conversation we were having? It's important for me to get this off my chest. Then…"

I hold my breath at his pause, equally terrified and excited about what he'll say next.

"…it's time we had a discussion."

6
ERIS

12 Years Old

Dolos launching the dish debris at me finally released the spell of shock my body was under. Doing my best to keep all my emotions from bursting out of me in front of him when he's already frightened, I school my facial features and move towards them to check on Mama.

I check her pulse first to make sure she's alive. Her heartbeat is thankfully strong but erratic. I let Dolos know before I begin scanning her body for other visible injuries.

The only thing we know is that she was holding her chest before she passed out. If something was wrong with her heart, I don't think it would still be beating as strongly as it is.

Scanning through the knowledge we've accumulated from Mama and Pop over the years, with the additions of our occasional tutors, my only options are a broken bond or a broken heart.

If something happened to Pop and he died…that could cause a broken bond, but that doesn't explain the yelling or smashed dishes.

I've never understood why fated mates were so important to people when this was the kind of partnership you could have. One where the man and father of the house is a total ass and doesn't have a caring bone in his body. *Is that what finding your mate does to men?*

I need to find out what happened.

Either something happened to Pop and thus, hurt Mama, or he…

Would he really?

Yes, I think he would.

If he's alive, he left her and rejected her, severing their bond.

If that's what happened, she's not out of the woods yet.

It was stressed in our studies that the pain of a severed mate bond can be fatal.

Allowing myself only a minute to watch where Dolos is curled around Mama, rubbing her lovingly, I turn on my heel and leave our home in the dead of night.

Mama and Dolos need me. I have to find out what happened.

I follow Pop's scent to either where he is or where he's been. There's a substantial lack of surprise when I'm led to a dingy-looking pub with drunk people hanging all over each other outside the building and staggering away. Unfortunately, one of those people is the man who gave me life.

Drawing in a breath to contain my rage, I approach where he's plastered against a tall woman with her legs wrapped completely around him. They're not only plastered together, but they're also sharing a sloppy, drunken kiss. This piece of shit is railing this woman, out in the open, minutes after destroying my mother's life.

"You," I growl, the sound coming out loud in the quiet night surrounding us. Even the bugs stop chirping, and the heads of many swaying bodies turn towards me, while a few take off.

We may only be twelve years old, but werewolves age much differently than humans. We're nearly fully grown by the time we're fourteen. I still have some growing to do, but my *father* raised me to be strong. He made sure I could both take a beating and deliver one…and that's exactly what

I intend to do.

He growls, removes himself from the woman, and turns toward me with drunken rage in his hooded eyes while he buttons his britches. "Get outta here. You're not my problem anymore." He chuckles with a look in his eyes that says he thinks he was able to hurt my feelings.

The bark of laughter that echos around us surprises him, and he pauses his retreat. Turning his face back to look at me—really look at me—his eyes narrowed in suspicion.

"I'm most definitely still your problem—though not the problem you were expecting, I'd presume," I scoff at him in a challenging voice.

Having his full attention, he takes a step towards me, pointing his crooked finger in my direction. The same finger he used as a lesson to teach us about how upsetting the wrong people can get you hurt. Seems the old man didn't learn his own lessons.

"Go back to your home and stay there. You won't be seeing me anymore. Not you. Not your worthless mother. And definitely not your idiot-fucking-brother," he yells into the night, causing the woman behind him to flinch and begin to move away.

Without any qualms of the consequences, I plow into him, slamming his body against the dingy pub by his neck. I'm vibrating with a level of anger I've never experienced before.

"The only worthless one here is you. But don't worry, *Pop*. You won't be seeing *anyone,* anymore, after tonight," I snarl into his ear so that only he can hear me.

"Beat it," I bark at the woman, who doesn't think twice before bolting away.

The alcohol on his breath is so strong that it makes my nose burn, and my eyes try to water. "Stop. Breathing." I growl as I continue to choke him, which would be much more difficult if he wasn't so fucking drunk.

Just before his eyes roll into the back of his head, I allow him enough oxygen to not pass out. I can't carry or drag the heavy bastard on my own, and we've already had too many witnesses. It needs to look as though I'm helping my drunken father return home.

Once we're out of sight of the pub and any lingering patrons, I redirect the course of our destination to the bridge over the dam between the villages to take care of this stain on our lives once and for all.

7
ERIS

Present

There was nothing I could do to prepare myself for what it would feel like to touch her. The tingling explosion of the mate bond. The depth of care reflected in her bright green eyes. I was drowning in her scent: vanilla, mint, and hope. When Dolos joined the embrace, the effects of the bond were somehow strengthened even further.

My knees buckled, my wolf howled, my fangs itched, and if I didn't get her out of my space, I was going to fuck her senseless and mark her, now. That couldn't happen, yet. *But fuck…I wanted it to.*

Everything suddenly made sense. Well, partially anyways. How the strongest and broodiest man I've ever met—my Alpha—could be turned into a pup by a woman. But if that's what a mate bond feels like, how can they mean so little to others?

Our father, Roman's father, and Khaos' father were all fortunate enough to be granted their fated mates, but they didn't care for them like they should have; they didn't appreciate them. Khaos' father cheated but stayed. Roman's father abused and killed. Our father cheated, abused, and left.

What determines which man you become when you find your mate and complete the bond? Is it the man or the bond? Would it be possible for my kind and happy brother to become something darker in the face of a bond? Or would he flourish and be the perfect mate while my darkness drowned them? What if I'm not good enough for her, for them? I don't want to taint their bond.

"Woah," Dolos breathes.

I wait, knowing his thoughts are about to catch up to his mouth and come pouring out any minute.

My heaving chest slows just as his eyes turn wide—*here we go*—"There's no way you didn't feel all of that. Eris..." His eyes pleading as he trails off.

We've never talked in depth about the thought of having mates. We were always adamant that we never wanted one after we saw the pain Mama went through to recover from the loss of hers, no matter how awful he was.

"Eris," he repeats.

Is he pleading that we complete the mate bond? Or is he pleading to understand?

I run my hands through my hair, growling as my wolf whimpers beneath my skin.

"There's something you don't know," I finally say through gritted teeth. I meant to tell him this so long ago. There was never a right time, and after long enough, it didn't matter anymore.

He stills, looking at me with a serious yet wary curiosity, and "What?" is all he asks.

I pace in front of the trunk at the foot of my bed, rearranging my thoughts so when they come out of my mouth, they make sense and deliver the least possible blow to my twin. It's not the act that I'm worried about him reacting to. It's the fact that I didn't tell him. It's the fact that I did it on my own; we have always done everything together…for the most part.

Finally stopping and dropping onto the trunk, I rest my elbows on the top of my thighs and catch my head in my hands. "I've tried to tell you this so many times," I begin.

Ever the attentive brother, Dolos dramatically lands on the floor, crosses his legs like a pup, and scoots closer to me with an obnoxious smile on his face, letting me know he's ready for whatever bomb I have to drop on him.

I try to smile back at him, but the muscles in my face feel rusty and unused. "Remember the night Pop left?"

Suspicion dances across his features briefly before he schools them and says, "Yep," popping the P.

"I went looking for him," I start again, preparing myself to tell my twin something that I buried deep ages ago. "We didn't know for sure what happened to him, and I wanted to know. He had either left Mama and severed their bond, or something happened to him, causing it to be severed. One way or another, I was going to find out. For Mama."

He nods, but doesn't say anything, so I continue.

"Well…I found him. Alive and well. Well, not entirely well. He was slobbering-fucking-drunk-wasted and sexually smothering a willing participant outside the pub."

His eyebrows scrunch together, and his previously relaxed stature hardens into one that reflects his temper that's beginning to simmer.

"When I confronted him, he didn't give a shit about any of us and basically told me to fuck off, and that he never had to see any of us again." The words send my blood boiling when I remember the way he spoke of my mother and brother. Words they will never know because it would needlessly hurt them.

He's just watching me when he finally says, "What does it matter what he said? We knew he left. We didn't need him back." There's a dejected tone in his voice that I hate. He knows how our father felt about him, and it's why I did what I did.

As quietly as I can, while still being heard, I allow myself to say the words I never thought I'd say.

8
DOLOS

12 Years Old

Mama sleeps for three whole days before she wakes up weak and disoriented, but alive. Eris and I have been taking shifts to make sure the chores stay done while we continue watching over her.

The strangeness that came over Eris the night it all happened has disappeared, and back is my animated and silly twin. The shift in him must have been a reaction to what was happening…or at least that's what I try to convince myself. Something very deep inside of me says it's something else, though.

I'm watching over her when she wakes, and she's visibly dizzy from sitting up. She instinctually looks over to the empty side of her bed, and a tear trickles down her soft cheek.

"It's okay, Mama. Eris and I will take care of you. We don't need him!" I encourage her with my smile that she says is her favorite.

Her teary eyes meet mine I worry that she'll miss him, that she'll want him back. So, I do the thing I'm good at. I keep smiling, and I keep talking. "Me and Eris have kept all the chores done, and one of us has been by your side since that night. You never have to worry about anything again, Mama." I beam at her and pray to the Goddess that she sends me a sign in the form of the tiniest smile on our sweet mother's face.

My prayers are answered when she nods to herself, straightens her shoulders, wipes her tears, and says, "You're right, sweet boy. We don't need him. I've got the two best men in the world right here."

And then she does it; she smiles big and bright. It's not even a fake smile like when you have to pretend. It's a sparkling smile, and I decide that if my mama can smile after what she's going through, there will never be a reason for me not to smile.

9
DOLOS

Present

"When I found him…I made sure he could never come back to hurt you or Mama…"

The words seep into my skin, running straight for my heart. There shouldn't be any pain for that monster. He was no father to Eris and me. He was a horrible mate to our mother. So why does my soul want to care? Why do I give a flying-fuck what happened to him? I knew he hated me, and still, there is an inkling of something inside of me that always wondered if he would come back for us. If he'd change his ways and decide to love us. Mama and I tried so hard to make him happy, happy enough that he would be like other mates who loved and cared for their family.

"Say something," Eris very quietly pleads.

I'm not usually at a loss for words, but I find myself searching the recesses of my brain trying to find the right thing to say. I'm not sure how I feel. *Do I congratulate him for slaying the evil villain of our childhood? Do I thank him for protecting me and Mama? Can I just nod?* I do just that…I just nod.

"Fuck, Dolos. He was a monster. He didn't deserve you or Mama. He was a fucking ass to both of you. I couldn't let him continue to hurt you. Even though he left, that wouldn't keep him from popping back in long enough to be an ass and leave…It wasn't worth the risk." His tone is dejected and wary…but he's absolutely correct.

If I were in his position, I would likely have done the same thing. Maybe not at twelve years old, but eventually…

"You did the right thing," is initially all I can manage while my brain and heart finally come to an agreement as they remember that Eris has always been built different under the lackadaisical skin he wore. I always knew; I just tucked it away for as long as he had.

"Does Mama know?" is the next thing that comes to mind.

He sadly shakes his head; not for what he did but for our sweet mother. "No, and I don't want her to. She moved on long ago, and I'd like to keep it that way."

Nodding to myself, I process the new information. While this is big news…it can't be the only thing that's been bothering him.

Our time in the King's Army was spent doing all levels of vicious things to get information and keep the kingdoms safe. The man that left us is not the only person to die by his hands. "What else is bothering you, dear brother?" I ask, pulling my charm back into place and relieving the previous shock of its duties.

Simultaneously, one of his eyebrows furrows, while the other raises. "That's all you have to say about what I just told you?"

I shake my head at him and offer him a sad smile. He kept this from me for centuries, worried about how I would react. "If I would have been as strong as you were at that age, I would have done the same thing," I tell him in all honesty.

I wish I would have been as strong as him in our youth. Maybe if I had been, Pop would have stayed for Mama. I don't care about him leaving Eris and me, but Mama deserved to be cherished. I hate that now that we're grown and gone, she lives alone. Granted, we moved her out of our little home in the middle of nowhere. We got her a new home on the outskirts of a bustling little village in the kingdom, closer to the castle, where she would be safe.

The emotion pouring off my brother is a triad of confusion, relief, and a miniscule amount of regret; surely not at what he'd done, but at not communicating this with me sooner.

"But what else is bothering you?" I press.

He continues scrubbing his hands over his face, his eyes full of a rare show of vulnerability. "What if I'm not a good mate?"

I'm unable to prevent my physical reaction to his words, jerking back in surprise where I sit in front of him. "Why the fuck would you think that?"

He's visibly searching his brain for the words to describe what he's feeling. "So many men we know had shit fathers. Shit fathers that were shit mates. What if I'm one of them? What if I'm one of the shit mates and fathers?"

Shaking my head in exasperation at the fact that he could ever think that, I say, "Eris…you're not. You're already so far from them." I try to console him, but it only seems to aggrevate him further.

"You don't know that! What about anything I've ever done in my fucking life says I would be anything more than a good fuck?" he roars.

I shouldn't laugh, I really shouldn't, but I can't help myself…and then I can't stop. By the time I get myself together, his eyes are full of fury and hurt.

"I'm so glad I can still amuse you," he rumbles, standing and walking to stare out his window, where he can see the wind move the snowy trees in the December sun.

Standing but not following him to the window, I elaborate, "Yeah, well, when you say dumb shit, there's a good chance I'm going to laugh at you. All those awful mates were also awful men. They didn't find their mate and magically turn into terrible creatures. Avram was always power hungry, so much that as a young man he went so far as to obtain an unlawful prophecy that we're now dealing with. Khaos' father came from a long line of lower-level royal douchery, from what I've heard. As for our father, Mama never had a nice family story to tell us about him. He never looked at her the way you just looked at Runa."

I pause to take a deep breath, "Not to mention, a man that was destined to be a shit mate would never have slain his own father to protect his mother and brother from an asshole. A man destined to be a shit mate would never have spent the next four years caring for his mother and brother as the man of the house when he was in fact the same age as his brother. A man who was destined to be a shit mate would not be worried about being a shit mate….and that's just the beginning of the list of reasons why you don't have to worry. I can continue if you like," I give him my orneriest smirk, but also hope he can see the love I have for him in my eyes, and feel it in our bond.

10
ERIS

Hearing how my twin sees me through his own eyes and experiences shatters the remaining shell from around my heart. "You really think all of that?"

His chuckle is a sad sound. "The only things you have in the 'con' column of this pros-and-cons list are the fact that you've buried this inside of you for so long, and the part where you kept your true self locked away from everyone...especially me," he scolds me lovingly, and as soon as he takes a step, I know what's coming.

"It's okay, you don't have to—" I'm cut off with an umph, and he plows into me and wraps me in a bone-crushing hug.

"TWIN HUG!" he sing-songs at the top of his lungs, and I hug him back. Any time we would fight as children, when the argument was over, this was basically the way he closed the door on the disagreement, and that meant it was over. The ritual unfortunately stuck and carried into our adult life. Luckily, we don't disagree much, so I've managed to avoid the act for quite some time.

"Alright, get off me, you lovey-dovey pain in my ass." My words don't have any venom in them, and he knows that. He squeezes my body one final time before pulling away.

"Now what?" he asks tentatively. He looks as though, if I said the words, he would be sprinting out of my room and collecting Runa for us to mate before lunch.

While that sounds like exactly what I'd like to do, I've learned from watching Roman and Leera that getting to truly know your mate makes for a much deeper connection. That's the kind of connection I want.

I want her to look at us the way Leera looks at Roman. I want to watch her eyes sparkle when we do something for her that she doesn't expect. I want her to know that she is irreplaceable and perfect.

"I've got an idea." I grin.

After I texted Khaos and Dolos texted Leera, we were able to sit down and make a plan. We got information about Runa and her favorite kinds of things from Khaos while gathering girly tips and tricks from our squealing Luna.

Yes, squealing. When Dolos texted her, she immediately called him, squealing and rambling information faster than he could write it down.

Her happiness flooded through the pack bond, filling us with her bubbly vigor. Having never felt something so light and feminine was an experience all on its own. Even our sweet Mama was not on Leera's level, granted, I don't think many people are. It's part of what makes her, her.

We brainstormed ideas and how to turn it all into one cohesive plan, and then we made lists. Two lists, to be exact. A list of things we needed to get and a list of things we needed to do. Then we split both lists in half so we each had things to get and do.

Lists in hand, we bolted out of the townhouse like it was on fire. Not entirely avoiding Runa, but I knew that if I saw her again before we were able to lay out the plan of what she deserves, I wouldn't be able to stop myself from claiming her unceremoniously in the living room.

11
Runa

My heart and wolf have been a raging mess since I threw myself at Eris, and he didn't push me away.

That was a good sign, right?

Did I do the wrong thing?

He hugged me back, didn't he?

Did I push him too far?

It's hard not to worry when they kicked me out—okay, they didn't actually kick me out; they politely asked me—to let them finish discussing something between themselves before we could all talk together. But then when I hear the door to Eris' room open, and I think we can finally talk, they practically sprint out of the house without even looking at me.

So, here I sit, stewing and insecure about what's going on.

Growing up in the strange and hidden way I did, I wasn't sure I'd ever find my mate. Because of that, I didn't have the silly little daydreams most females do. They fantasize about what the moment their mate notices them will be like. They dream of how he'll claim her. They manifest all the qualities their future mate will possess.

After what my mother went through…I wasn't sure I wanted a mate. I was born in secret and smuggled out of our realm in hiding so that I was given the chance to even *live* because of my mother's fated mate.

Even seeing members of the pack find their mates didn't assuage my lack of interest. It was better I stay to myself. Stay happy. Stay safe.

Who would have thought that my *mates* would have been here with my brother almost the whole time.

Have they been waiting for me? Looking for me?

The worry in my mind can't seem to be quieted, so I decide I might as well go for a run. Maybe if I let my wolf loose for a bit, some of this anxiousness can dissipate.

Stretching first, then rising from my seat on the couch, I make my way to the main door of the townhouse. I reach to hit the button to the elevator, only to realize I can already hear the whirring of the motor moving it…up, towards me.

My initial reaction is to dart away, pretend to be uninterested and collected, but who am I kidding? That's not me right now.

My feet are locked in place when the elevator doors slowly slide open, revealing my twin mates. Dolos is smiling wide with sparkling eyes, while one look at Eris nearly knocks me off my feet. He's not frowning, and his eyes are warmer than I've ever seen them. They both look like an awkward mixture of excited and nervous, but I'll take this over the tormented, defeated, and sorrowful looks from before.

My jaw must have been hanging open because Dolos takes a step towards me and lovingly lifts my jaw back into a more natural place. I shake myself from my stupor as he chuckles.

"Runa," Eris breathes my name.

It's going to take me a lifetime to get used to the fact that he's finally speaking to me. He looks like he's struggling to get the rest of his words out, so Dolos butts in, "Can we take you on a date?"

The question is so unexpected that I rear back slightly, almost giggling before I catch the guarded expression on Eris' face.

They're serious, and he thinks I'll decline.

"This isn't some kind of trick, is it? You're actually"—I look at each of them—"asking me out on a date?"

Dolos nods theatrically, which makes me smile, but my eyes move over to Eris, who looks to be searching for his words.

After what feels like a century, he speaks cautiously with a hopeful look in his eyes, "We've learned much from our Luna," he begins, thinking far too hard about his words as he says them. "Watching the way she and Roman courted each other before completing their mate bond was eye-opening. We thought we didn't want a mate…" Eris trails off.

My heart drops into my stomach.

"But we decided now that we have one, she should feel just as loved and cherished as our Luna. If we're going to try to do this…" Dolos continues.

My heart retakes its place in my chest where it belongs.

"We want to do it right," Eris says with a gentle finality. "It's gonna be all or nothing with us, Precious."

"Precious?" I whisper out loud, more to myself.

"Mmhmm," Eris grunts to confirm.

I'm standing here processing everything they said while they wait for an answer. As much as I want to scream "yes" and jump into their arms, I still feel the need to leave a small protective layer around my heart. There's no reason for them to go from zero contact for weeks to taking me on a date in a complete one-eighty so unexpectedly…

There's got to be something they still haven't told me.

Their energies shift from optimistic to something more like worry.

"On one condition." The words leave me far more confidently than I expected. I thank the Goddess for loaning me some courage and calmly cross my arms over my chest with a calm and accepting expression on my face. "First, I want to know everything."

12
DOLOS

Well, shit.

This is not how this was supposed to go.

The plan we carefully concocted was to take her on a date, get her all buttered up, and *then* tell her everything.

What do we do now? Eris grouses through our link. Clearly irritated with me that our plan didn't go according to plan. Like I had any idea this would happen.

My shoulders slump as I consider our options.

The most logical option to most people would be to give her a half-baked version of the truth to pacify her until we're comfortable telling her the whole thing. The alternate—and I think most responsible—option is to rip off the proverbial band-aid and give the lady what she wants.

Her dispute from when she laid us all bare to Roman come to me. "If I'm going to be getting to know my brother and creating a life here, I won't start it with half-truths..."

We have to tell her, I elaborate my internal dialogue, explaining my reasoning, and I can see the moment he knows that's what we have to do.

He rebuilds the wall around his heart brick-by-brick for fear that after we tell her, she'll reject him. What he doesn't know is that…if she rejects him over this…she'll be rejecting me too.

I won't take a mate that rejects my twin brother. No matter how badly it hurts. We're a package deal. In my heart, I believe that we're two halves of the same soul, and I will not allow him to be cast aside for doing what he felt was right to protect those he loved.

13
ERIS

Well, fuck.

All that time we spent planning…for possibly nothing.

This whole mess is one spark away from going up in flames, engulfing the three of us in an inferno, along with our chances of her accepting us… and by us, I mean me.

After Dolos insists we tell her the truth with sound reasoning, I offer her a curt nod.

She seems to have deflated a fraction as she leads us to the strangely quiet living room. It's weird to be here while everyone is gone.

As we approach the large couch, I worry that this is it. That it will all come tumbling down around me before I ever get a chance to try and prove myself.

She takes a seat in the center of the couch. Dolos plops down on the end. I can't sit. My nerves are like live wires, dancing around my body looking for a source to ground them. For that reason, I remain standing, pacing a small path in the floor while they watch. Neither rush me nor seem irritated with my need to move.

After a few more laps, I feel like the electricity in my limbs is more contained, and I stop. Still standing, because I don't think I could sit still, I nod to Dolos. "Start at the beginning. Tell her everything. I'll add my perspective when it's needed."

Two hours later, we've told her almost everything and answered all of her questions as we went, instead of saving them all for the end. Up to this point, she's been very receptive and understanding, having come from a less-than-ideal start to life herself, but I don't know how far that sympathetic attitude will extend. Not many people—werewolves or other—are necessarily okay with murder, no matter the justification.

"Today, I learned," Dolos continues, looking at me with questioning eyes, *You ready?*

I nod. *As ready as I'm going to be.* I sit on the other end of the couch from Dolos, sandwiching her in, and preparing myself for the worst as Dolos tells her his side of that night, leading up to mine.

My fists clench and unclench in my lap. I watch her take in every word with openness and concern etched in her features. *Is that concern for us and Mama? Or concern for where this is going?*

Resting my elbows on the top of my thighs and hanging my head, I attempt to steady my breathing in preparation for what I have to tell the only woman that can break me.

I feel both their eyes on me when Dolos finishes his monologue, and they redirect their attention to me. Not even lifting my head, far too terrified to watch her face morph into disgust and rejection. With one final inhale and long exhale, I tell her everything. Just as I told Dolos.

When the final words leave my lips, I realize I'm shaking. I've never really been afraid of anything in my existence. I learned early on that fear only gave things more power over you. Therefore, I didn't allow myself to feel fear. I pushed myself to analyze my doubts and concerns and adapted potential fears into things I challenged myself to overcome, vowing not to let them consume me.

"I'll understand if it's too much for you…I…you deserve so much more…I-I'm sorry."

Preparing myself for her rejection, I squeeze my eyes shut, praying to the Goddess to give me even the smallest chance. Let me take care of her. Let me love her.

Lost in my worry and newfound fear, I'm surprised by her vanilla-mint scent overwhelming my senses a fraction of a second before she drops into the space between my legs.

Her incredibly soft, gentle hands cup my face, lifting it so that I'm forced to meet her watery green eyes.

Her eyes volley between mine. I brace for impact when her lips twitch, ever so slightly.

I'm too stunned to realize that she's crashed her mouth against mine, pulling away too soon. She scolds me between slamming kisses against my lips, "You. Stupid. And. Beautiful. Man."

Opening my eyes to watch her and make sure I'm not dreaming, I find her playfully glaring at me with a watery smile on her face. "Please tell me there's more. Please tell me this isn't the reason you've kept yourselves from me?" she asks in disbelief.

My brows crease in confusion; unable to find my words, I nod full of apprehension.

"Eris." She rests her soft hand on my face once more, and I can't help but lean into. "You've met my father. How could you possibly think I would hold such an act against you?" She shakes her head at me with the softest smile, glancing over her shoulder to Dolos.

"Seriously, boys?" she asks, looking between us again, "Is that really all it is? You're not secret serial killers or human traffickers or something, are you?" she asks in jest, but I can see the underlying seriousness.

"None of the above, Precious," I vow.

14
Runa

These ornery, stubborn, beautifully tormented men. To think they genuinely thought I wouldn't want them over him killing a monster of a mate and father to protect his mother and brother.

I've literally dreamt of doing such a thing myself, but my mother is long past the ability to be saved.

When they finished their detailed explanations of that night, I expected so much worse than the reality they presented, and I couldn't stop myself from physically reacting.

I can't stop myself from shaking my head at them. "Then, what are we waiting for?" I ask quietly, worried I'll break the blissful peace in the room.

Eris lifts me from the floor and pulls me into his lap crashing his lips against mine. I open for him without hesitation, and the invitation doesn't go unanswered. His tongue delves into my mouth, leaving none of it untouched by him.

My hands are wrapped around his neck, and I run my nails along his tender skin, treasuring the feeling of the goosebumps that rise in their path.

The couch dips behind me as I feel Dolos sit next to us. His hand starts tracing patterns on my back, and I'm consumed by the current of our mate bond as it thrums between us.

Eris' hands move from where they were holding my face to right where he wanted me. He clings to my ass cheeks before he begins kneading the flesh there. The moan that escapes me conveys the weeks of wanting that have been coursing through my body.

With my face no longer held in place, I break our kiss and turn to Dolos. He answers my call without me having to mutter even a sound. His lips don't crash into mine, though. They caress. They indulge. They consume.

Are they also opposites in the way they touch and love?

When I grind my hips on Eris, whimpering into Dolos' mouth, both men halt their movements, all of us panting.

My confusion must be written all over my face, because they soften when they notice. Dolos trails his fingers down my cheek. Eris holds onto my hips, offering me a squeeze and a smirk when Dolos finally speaks up, "We wanted to make our mating special for you…like Roman and Leera," he begins.

"Hence the request for a date," Eris completes the thought.

My mouth forms a small "O" as the blush rushes to my cheeks.

"But we can forget all of that if it's that important to you," Dolos blurts nervously causing Eris to elbow him, both of them laughing.

"We can," Eris growls and glares at his brother. "Although we'd truly like to take this one step at a time, we won't change our mind if that's what worries you." He finishes softly, and I think that's exactly what it was… other than being all worked up, of course. I was afraid that if I didn't get their marks immediately, they'd have time to change their minds.

After offering each one what I hope is a loving look, I nod, then glance between them suspiciously because I'm fairly certain they're communicating without me right now.

"But," they say in unison.

"We can't have our mate feeling unsatisfied, Eris," Dolos says dramatically, my head whipping back to Eris' face when he says, "We most certainly cannot."

If my panties hadn't been wet before, that would have been all I needed to be ready for them.

Dolos gets up from the couch first, walking toward his room. I move to stand from Eris' lap, but his hold on my ass tightens as he rises fluidly, showing no signs that my additional weight slowed him in the least.

Taking advantage of my position, I take his rough face back in my hands and resume my exploration of his mouth, all while he moves us to Dolos' room, right next to his.

Once we're mated...will I have to alternate staying in each room? I don't think I'll be able to stand being away from one of them once I have them. Why these thoughts are plaguing me now, I don't know.

Once through the door, Dolos shuts it even though we're the only one's home, and Eris carries me to the bed. I expect him to toss me onto it, but the level of care in which he sets me down has my eyes glossing.

My need for them is overwhelming my senses. Dolos takes over, kissing me senseless. *Where did Eris go?* I've never had more than one man, and I was not prepared for this. When I have one's full attention, I still find myself looking for the other.

My thoughts are answered when I feel my jeans being unbuttoned, and the throbbing between my thighs increases with him that close. He seems to be being careful not to touch me yet as he removes my pants with surgical precision.

I'm trying to rub my thighs together to gather some kind of friction when he pushes my legs apart and groans before sliding my underwear off.

"Dolos, come see how wet she is for us," he instructs his twin with no room for argument. Dolos' lips leaving mine causes me to whimper as he moves to the foot of the bed, and they both watch me.

The thing is, I've been alone a long time. I know how to please myself. Lifting my torso from the bed, I pull my shirt and sports bra off in one motion, leaving myself bare to them.

The lust in their eyes causes me to moan as they watch me. Lifting my hand to my face, I suck my finger into my mouth before trailing it across my collarbone and down to my breast, plucking on my already peaked nipple.

They still don't move. Totally bewitched by…me…

I move my hand lower, lazily tracing my curves, the tops of my thighs, and then my center. Lightly rolling my clit in circles, I let my head fall back, and my body heats under their eyes and my touch.

"Stop." Eris' gravelly voice barks somewhere between a request and a command.

My movements still, but I don't pull my hand away just yet. Lifting my eyes, I make eye contact with Dolos first, then Eris, silently asking, "why?"

"Let us take care of you, Darling," Dolos purrs, and what girl could say no to that?

I can still have a little fun with them, though. "And how do I know you can *take care of me* efficiently?" I ask as sensually as I can.

They prowl towards me, moving up the bed in unison. It's incredibly sexy and slightly intimidating until I realize, "You're still clothed," I whine.

"Today is about you, Precious," Eris informs me.

"But—" I try to complain, but Dolos silences me with another kiss.

Consumed by their scents on either side of me, my wolf is preening. Bonfires and an autumn breeze on my right. Blooming trees and spring rain on the other. It doesn't help that their scents have taken on the muskier additions of their arousal, making me crave them even more.

Dolos kisses me slowly, and he angles my head to allow Eris to kiss, nibble, and suck on my neck. When both of their hands finally touch my bare flesh, my back bows off the bed at the sensation of our mate bond calling out to us.

We're a moaning, groaning, writhing mess as they kiss and tease me and pay special attention to my breasts.

Completely in sync, they rotate their positions. Eris taking over my lips while Dolos moves towards my neck; all the while, their hands continue to descend my body.

I'm not prepared for the impact of our bond when the skin of their hands makes contact with my most sensitive flesh. Calling out, Eris begins rubbing my clit while Dolos slides a finger into me. Their motions have the pleasure climbing higher and higher within me when suddenly, they stop.

"Wha—" I start.

"Shhh," they interrupt.

Eris wastes no time licking two fingers and slowly sliding them inside me, curling them and massaging my inner walls when Dolos asks, "Has anyone ever had you here?" as he smears my wetness from his fingers to my rear hole.

I wriggle my body against them, overwhelmed by all the sensations. "Answer me, Darling," Dolos demands.

"No," I breathe.

"Yessss," he hisses at my response, clearly happy that they'll be the only ones to have that piece of me.

They continue to work my body while having another obvious conversation without me.

"Right," Dolos suddenly leaps off the bed and makes his way towards his dresser. Returning a moment later, he explains, "We better start training you now, then," he says matter-of-factly, like everything he says just makes sense.

"T-training me?" I ask as Eris removes his fingers from inside me, licking my slick from his fingers, a wicked grin spreading across his beautifully handsome face as he nods.

"For us to claim you properly, you must be knotted by both of us at the same time while we mark you, Precious," he reminds me.

Holy shit. I had been so worked up over if they'd ever claim me that I hadn't even thought about how that would work with two mates. "Will it hurt?"

"Of course not. We'd never hurt you. That's why we have to train you. Stretching you a little more each time so that it's only pleasurable," Dolos tells me as he pumps a small drop of clear liquid on his finger. He brings his finger toward my body, generously applying the lubrication to the area before going back for another smaller pump and covering his index finger in it. "Okay, brother. Resume," he tries to say seriously but breaks off in a chuckle.

Surprisingly, Eris does what his twin says without balking at being told what to do. He immediately resumes the glorious work on my body that has me panting immediateley.

As Dolos lies next to me, he pulls his foot towards his body, lifting his knee as he picks up my left leg and rests it on top of his thigh, opening me for him. His hand glides across my skin, and when he reaches my puckered hole, he isn't met with resistance. Thanks to the lube, he gently inserts the tip of his finger, and I cry out, surprised at how much stronger it heightens the feel of the work Eris is doing to my clit.

"Oh, Goddess!" My body grinds against them, all of our bodies moving in tandem. My movements have driven Dolos' finger further inside of my ass, and as he does, he continues to move, stretching me and firing off explosive shocks of pleasure straight to my clit that Eris has decided to massage with his talented tongue.

"More. Harder. Shit, I don't know!" I pant, and my words become an incoherent mess of shouting as they continue to praise my body with their hands, tongues, and words. "I'm…Oh, fuck! Eris! Dolos!" I scream as my body implodes around them.

15
DOLOS

She's so bloody perfect, I say to Eris when sleep immediately consumes Runa. Both of us having already grabbed a warm rag from our jack-and-jill bathroom to gently clean her up before tucking her into my bed. There's no telling how long she'll sleep with how stressed we've had her lately.

Who says bloody? Eris scoffs back.

Well, mostly the Brits, but sometimes I like to spice things up. Why haven't you noticed this, big brother? I ask, offering him an obnoxious smile that he responds to by shoving me in the shoulder.

Be nice to me, or I'll kick you out of my room, I threaten, sticking my tongue out at him.

We both return to our mate, settling in on each side of her perfect, still-naked body. Neither of us says a word out loud or through our link. Our eyes trace her face, memorizing every inch and committing it to memory.

The way she seems to be almost smiling in her sleep. The way she curls up on her side, bringing her knees up in front of her. The way her shallow breaths barely blow the hairs on my chest. The way I have never felt more content in all of my existence than I do right now, by her side.

After what could have been either fifteen minutes or two hours, I break the silence, "Well, now that our date idea got trashed so wonderfully, what should we do?"

He doesn't answer me immediately; his own eyes continue to catalog her every movement and detail, so I don't interrupt him. Instead, I watch him watch her. Chuckling at myself when my internal dialogue makes me realize how weird that would have sounded had I said it out loud.

"We let her tell us in her own way," he answers me, his voice heavy with the exhaustion he too must be feeling. I know he hasn't been sleeping. Even when he puts up his mental walls, I can feel his restlessness. Even when he pretends everything is fine, I can tell when he's struggling.

I like to let him believe that I only know him as the big, strong, only-slightly-older brother that he is when, in reality, I can tell when he needs my joviality to keep him from succumbing to the darkness that has always resided within him.

I decide not to push him on what he means by letting her tell us. Instead, I also allow myself to rest my head on my hand, with my elbow propped on the bed. Watching my brother finally close his eyes and fall into sleep, I watch the two of them for a few more minutes, soaking up the surreal feeling of having my entire world in one space.

Finally.

With my heart full and my mind open, I follow them into sleep.

16
ERIS

Only when my hazy awareness turns into full-blown consciousness do I realize that I've slept. I didn't doze in and out of an almost-sleep like I normally would; I actually slept. Hard. I'd forgotten what real sleep even felt like.

Opening my eyes, I look for the source of the strangely perfect weight resting against my body. Yesterday's events flood my mind and bring me a level of peace I've never known.

Finally telling my brother what I did all those years ago and for him to be not only accepting of the information but also almost…proud of it in a way that felt like he wished he had taken the action himself, but I never wanted that for him.

It's not like the work we did for the military. Monster or not, that man was our father. He was the one who gave us life. I did what I had to do, but it wasn't easy.

Runa makes a nonsensical sound in her sleep, bringing my attention back to a moment I didn't think I'd ever get to experience. Waking with my mate in my arms. I draw her body closer to mine. Even though she was only a whole inch away, I need to feel her heartbeat against my skin. My wolf is a level of calm I've rarely experienced within me, and a sigh of…happiness—yeah, that's definitely happiness—leaves me.

In his sleep, Dolos follows her, her body now pressed tightly between us, and fuck if I can't wait to claim her. But that has to wait. Seeing everything Roman has done for Leera, I want those reactions. I want our mate to be happy beyond words. I want her to know she wants us without a doubt, not only because of the bond.

Dolos stirs, slowly waking. He sleepily takes in the scene laid out across his bed, and, like me, looks like he was worried it was all a dream or hallucination. But she's here. She's still sleeping heavily between us. She's all golden skin with a few scattered dark-brown freckles, or maybe they're tiny moles. No matter what they are, they make up the most beautiful constellation that is our mate.

My twin's hand begins to trace the same route my eyes were just following, a path of goosebumps lifting on her skin, but she remains deeply slumbering. Dolos' eyes meet mine and a wicked grin spreads across his face. Raising an eyebrow, I watch as he lifts his body from the bed, allowing Runa to slowly roll onto her back.

He moves himself to the end of the bed, positioning himself in line with her body, and slowly moves back up towards her.

What are you doing? I snap at him, but he doesn't slow or change his trajectory.

I want to taste her, he says plainly, like I should have known what he intended to do.

I probably should have. I blame my brain acclimating to my sudden ability to sleep.

Watching as he moves her left leg to the side, I help him, moving her right leg and hooking it over my body. He settles between her spread thighs, taking a large inhale of her intoxicating, vanilla-mint scent.

When his tongue meets her already glistening center, a heady sigh leaves her as she remains asleep, my dick hardening against her thigh I'm still holding. He begins to work her in long, languid strokes, enough for her body to know what's happening, but not enough to wake her. To add to the building pleasure in her body, I softly trace circles around her nipples, grazing my fingers over the pebbled peaks.

Her back slightly arches off the bed, and I think she'll wake, but her eyes are dancing behind her lids. She's dreaming of the sensations overcoming her. I continue to watch her face, waiting for the moment she wakes as the strokes of his tongue become more urgent.

"Eris…Dolos…" she breathes heavily in her pleasure-addled dream state, and fuck if I don't almost shoot my load as Dolos groans against her sensitive flesh. Knowing she's dreaming of us sends a shiver of possessiveness down my spine, my gums itching to claim her, but not yet.

Locking eyes with Dolos, I nod, and we decide it's time for our perfect little mate to wake up and join the fun. He slowly gives her two fingers in her swollen pink center and latches onto her clit, sucking on it, while I use both hands to knead and pinch her nipples.

She wakes with a loud gasp as she rises onto her elbows, taking in the scene with lust-hooded eyes. "Oh, fuck," she throws her head back and moans, "I was…dreaming," she pants, "Goddess," she begins to work her body, riding Dolos' face and fingers. "You—Oh!" She gives up on talking and lets us wake her the way she deserves.

"She's close, fuck, I can feel her locking around my fingers," Dolos mumbles against her as he consumes her completely, before we stop in sync.

Still braced on her elbows, her head flies up, eyes wild with need. "Wh-why did you stop?" she cries.

Dolos makes a show of licking his face and fingers while we move around the bed, switching positions. She watches our every move, especially as I grab the lubricant from the side table while he begins plucking her still sensitive nipples.

"I ahhh…I'm feeling very underdressed," she whines, lifting her body into my twin's touch, squirming on the bed, searching for friction.

With calm movements and matching grins, we remove our clothing for her, our cocks springing free of their confines. Her eyes drink us in, and she whimpers at the sight of us. Dolos is now at her right, and she reaches for him, wrapping her delicate fingers around his length without hesitation, and he hisses through his teeth at the contact.

My cock is so hard it hurts. I add a few drops of the lube to my hand, slowly stroking myself a few times, her eyes volleying between us. When she's decided we've gone too long without touching her, she starts to move her free hand to take care of herself.

"Tsk, tsk, tsk, that's our job now," I growl with a small smile on my face.

She smiles back with a challenge in her eyes, darting her tongue out to lick Dolos' swollen tip. "Well then, you better take your job more seriously so I don't have to do it for you," she teases, her hand relentlessly continuing its path to her sex. Instead of pleasuring herself, though, she simply holds herself open for me. Waiting for me to take control.

"Yes, ma'am," we groan in unison, Dolos' head tipped back, eyes closed as she continues to gently stroke him, now peppering kisses along his shaft.

Generously applying the bottle's contents to her ass and my fingers, I don't waste time inserting my first finger as she moans and clenches around me. Leaning in, I kiss the inside of her thigh before latching onto her skin and sucking hard. She'll only have a mark for a couple hours at most, but it'll still be there.

When she's finally begun to relax around my finger, I work the second into her tight hole. She gasps as she watches my movements, my eyes locking on hers as she absentmindedly strokes Dolos.

"Are you okay?" I breathe.

She doesn't answer, but she nods, her bottom lip between her teeth as she whimpers. Leaning in further, while I work in my second finger, I softly, reverently massage her throbbing clit with my tongue. She melts against me, relaxing almost instantly, allowing me to slowly pump both lubricated fingers in her ass.

"What a good mate you are." I kiss her clit, inserting my thumb into her pussy, her eyes rolling momentarily before returning to my gaze.

Ready to make her come, I ask my brother. He leans back over her, massaging one breast while pinching the other nipple, then alternating his movements. My fingers massage her holes while my tongue works her clit. The taste of her flooding my senses as she gasps, pants, moans, and erratically strokes Dolos—who is also now grunting, close to his release.

She comes first, I remind him, and he nods in understanding.

When her body continues to clench and tighten her muscles around me, I double my efforts until she collapses off her elbows, screaming our names moments before Dolos roars her name, ropes of cum painting her torso. I continue to massage her through the waves of her orgasm, making sure she gets every ounce of pleasure she deserves.

"Okay…ah, Eris…it's t-too much," she moans, still writhing and twitching from her release. I gently remove my fingers, watching her face for a wince or flinch that I went too far, but she doesn't. She simply sinks into the bed and sighs dreamily, "A girl could get used to this."

Dolos outright laughs, "That's kind of the point, Darling," then drops a dramatic kiss to her lips before standing with his hands on his hips, taking in the scene of her thoroughly pleasured and covered in his cum. "Runa, you were fantastic. Ten out of ten. Would recommend."

She barks a laugh and covers her face with her hands while I shake my head at him as I head to the bathroom for more warm, wet washcloths to take care of our mate.

17
Runa

A blissful and strangely normal day was exactly what I needed.

The twins and I spent the day together doing nothing other than occasionally pleasuring each other…with the exception of Eris.

The stubbornness in that man runs deeper than I ever knew possible. While we'd made these monumental steps towards our relationship—the three of us—he still had things he seemed to be holding back. I don't know if he is still worried I might change my mind and reject him, but he claims to just be old-fashioned in some weird ways.

He won't let me touch him the way Dolos lets me. I've felt Dolos, and I've tasted him. Eris won't let me…yet. He *claims* that when he comes for me for the first time, he wants it to be when he claims me. I've never heard of such a tradition among any wolves, so it must just be him.

Nevertheless, it doesn't take away from the surprisingly perfect day. We lounged around, we snacked and ordered take out. We watched some television, but mostly, we just talked. About everything. Growing up. Their lives after leaving their mother and Zabella. Hockey. The pack. Everything.

I vaguely remember Leera telling me that she and Roman had a similar, and also much-needed, day to themselves after her first heat.

I *so* wasn't looking forward to going into heat. Sure, I had double the amazing mates to handle me sexually and get me through it, but Leera says the need rises so high that it's almost painful, and *that* sounds awful.

After another round of Dolos and me getting off and Eris making sure I saw stars but not letting me reciprocate, we're lying sprawled across Eris' bed. They bickered that we spent last night in Dolos' room and that we should stay in his tonight. Logic won, and here we lie. Spent and happy, if only slightly contemplative.

How will this work between the three of us? I thought to myself, my wolf huffing at me like she was saying, *How the fuck am I supposed to know?* And I giggled out loud at her.

"What's so funny?" Eris grumbled, and with my head resting on his chest, I could feel the vibrations begin in my skull and skitter through my body to my toes.

"My wolf," was all I gave them for now.

How could I tell them the things slap-shotting through my brain?

Would they always bicker over where we slept, passing me back and forth like a custody agreement?

Was there enough space in one of the rooms for us to all be together?

Did they even want to spend that much time with each other?

Are either of them jealous or upset that they have to share me?

Did they want pups?

If we had a family, would they be jealous over who fathered pups?

My worries began consuming me in a way I wasn't used to. I'd never had a real family before. Therefore, I never had things like this to worry about. I hadn't been sure I'd ever find my mate because I didn't think I'd ever leave Khaos' pack lands.

The onslaught of…well…everything was just so much sometimes, and I had no idea how Leera handled the mess that had recently become her life—her words, not mine.

"Penny for your thoughts?" Dolos asked softly, twirling a strand of my dark hair around his fingers. The way he looks at me will take some getting used to. He's so soft and gentle with me. Like he too is afraid I might bolt, but he handles that worry differently than his brother.

I consider how to answer his question without word-vomiting the mess of my thoughts across our peaceful space. "I hadn't realized how much there is to consider with our…particular mating situation." I try to laugh it off, but I can hear the nerves in my voice, so I know they did too.

"What are your concerns?" Eris demands. Direct as always. A man of few words, and he doesn't candy-coat anything. I mostly love it. It's refreshing for someone to be so honestly themselves. I realize I don't think I would have liked the Eris that Leera met—the one that matched Dolos. I like this Eris. My Eris.

Sitting up on the bed and crossing my legs, I fiddle with the edge of the sheet crumpled beneath us. I make the decision to continue to let them in. We're building this muddle on honesty and communication, so clamming up now wouldn't be helpful. "Well…let's start with living arrangements. I get that we'll be staying here…for some time at least, but—"

"We were considering tearing down the walls between our rooms and moving the bathroom to create one large space," Dolos jumps in to elaborate with that oversized smile on his face. "If that sounds like something you'd like."

Nodding my head as I consider his words, that makes sense. I would definitely rather us be together. Once we've marked each other, I can't imagine spending a night away from either of them. "So, this"—I wave my hands between the three of us—"doesn't bother you? Having to share me?"

Eris barks a laugh that startles me at the abruptness of it. He calms me by rubbing soothing, and slightly arousing, circles on my hips. "The majority of women we gave any time to before we shared."

I shouldn't feel jealous over things that came before me—*women* that came before me—but I can't help the itch of jealousy gnawing at my skin. The thought of them touching anyone else spreads through me, also irritating my wolf. The thought of them smiling at anyone else has my claws elongating and an unbidden growl leaving my lips.

"Easy, Precious. We are yours. Completely." Eris strokes my cheek, one side of his lips tilting in an ornery grin. "Though I'd be lying if I said I didn't like you all jealous and worked up over it," he finishes, lifting the other side of his lips into a full smile that steals the air from my lungs and deflates my rage.

With my main concerns thwarted, I return to my comfortable position between them, where I can touch them both. I can't stop touching them. Staring at the ceiling as the sky outside shifts colors while the sun sinks and the moon rises, we continue just talking. Just being together.

I'd never before enjoyed any male's presence the way I craved being around Eris and Dolos. I was bingeing myself on them with absolutely no desire to stop. I could listen to them talk forever, even after a full day's worth.

We discussed music and movies and trashy TV shows. They told me stories about hockey, and I told them about Khaos as an Alpha.

They took turns telling me about missions they went on for the King's army with my brother as their commander, while I told them about my adoptive family.

I asked about the things that made them happy and the things they still wanted to do. I told them about the things I still wanted to see and do—Leera had called it a bucket list when we had had a similar conversation.

I learned that Dolos' favorite color is a dusty-turquoise, while Eris' is a dark teal—again, the same but relatively opposite. Their favorite colors reminded me of a postcard I used to have, pulling me into my memories.

One of the women in our pack had decided to take a trip around the human realm, sending us postcards as she went—back when postcards were still a popular thing you didn't have to explain to people.

My favorite was the one she sent back of an island in Hawaii. The waves of the water. The foliage in every shade of green. It was stunning, and a piece of my heart always dreamed of going there.

I told them all of this when they told me their favorite colors, letting my heart remember how I'd felt the first time I'd seen that postcard.

When they asked my favorite color in return, though…I wasn't sure. I'd never really been asked that. There was never really room in my life for a lot of color...or people. So, I said the only thing I could think of. The color that now brought me the most happiness when I thought of it.

"Gray." I had said, and their features softened. The colors of their eyes. The colors of their wolves. The colors of my mates.

18
DOLOS

"We have a surprise for you!" I hollered as soon as we returned home and walked through the elevator door.

It had taken an entire day of distracting Runa and organizing to make it happen, but now that it's all ready to go, I am bursting at the seams with excitement. Eris is too; he just isn't showing it.

Runa comes down the hallway wearing a suspicious smile. Her dark brown hair is tied in twin braids framing her perfect face, her bright green eyes blazing with curiosity. Leaning against the wall at the end of the hall, she crosses her arms over her chest, wearing only my white Predators T-shirt; the white a stark contrast to her dark golden skin.

She doesn't say anything, just raises an eyebrow with a smirk, waiting for me to tell her, but she isn't getting off that easy.

"Pack your bags. Necessities. We'll get everything else we need when we get there," Eris clips, not giving anything away. I'm too worried if I open my mouth, the entire surprise will come spilling out and ruin the look on her face when we get there.

Confusion continues to mar her face, her arms falling slack at her sides as she stares at us, expecting more information than the dubious instructions Eris dropped at her feet when he kept walking right past her to his room. Following his lead, I head in her direction, but I can't help but to stop and slam my lips to hers for just a moment before I head to my room to pack my own bag of necessities.

She whirls around in the spacious hallway, and I can't help but to shut my door, laughing the whole time. I know that if she gets her hands or lips on me, I won't be able to hold it in, and I don't want to be the surprise ruiner today.

She tries the doorknob, and when she realizes I've locked it, she scoffs at me, bangs on it once, and heads for Eris' door. His opens, and I hear her shouting at him for information until her words are cut off, and I can practically feel her need from here. Whether he's touching her or just kissing her, he's got her distracted for a second at least.

The quiet only lasts a minute, though, as she makes an adorable screeching noise at him before she stomps past our rooms and back to hers—hopefully to pack like we asked her to.

With our bags at our feet, we stand in the foyer waiting for her to come down with her own. After a few minutes, I get antsy, so I rummage through the fridge for a snack and something to drink. Eris is also starting to get nervously agitated but won't admit it, so he just keeps checking his watch. I don't know why. He hired a private jet, so it's not like we're gonna miss our flight or anything.

Just as he drops his hand with a scoff, she finally emerges, lugging two overstuffed bags of what can't possibly all be necessities, causing me to lose control of the laughter that quickly climbs up my throat. "Those are all necessities, Darling?"

Her eyes shoot daggers at me across the space as her cheeks pink with blush. "I've never really gone on a spontaneous trip before…I've never really gone on *any* trip before. I didn't know what to pack, especially without knowing where we are going," she finishes as she watches her toes kick lightly at her bags now resting on the floor by her feet, looking embarrassed. Eris growls at me through our bond for making her feel that way.

He approaches her slowly, but she doesn't look up at him. Curling his hand around her jaw, his thumb rubbing her chin, he kisses her on the forehead before he lifts her eyes to his. "Ignore him, Precious. Are you ready to go?" he purrs at her, instantly melting her rigid posture, shoulders loosening and no longer at her ears.

She nods, offering him a weak smile, then leans in and kisses him on the cheek, and…I'll be damned…my big, grumpy brother smiles and may have just blushed a bit himself.

Fully scolded, I approach her, nuzzling the top of her head and whispering into her hair, "I'm sorry for being insensitive."

She nods into my embrace, wrapping her arms around me before Eris disengages her from me and effortlessly lifts her into his arms, making her squeal with laughter. "You get the bags, brother. I got the important stuff." He tosses her over his shoulder as he makes his way to the door.

Laughing, I do as I'm told and collect our bags before hurrying after them.

19
ERIS

After trying for nearly an hour to get us to tell her where we are going, Runa finally gave up and allowed herself to rest. We planned and boarded a flight that would allow us to sleep overnight through the nine-and-a-half-hour trip, hopefully timing it just right so that when we arrive, the sun will be rising.

Knowing that I've been sleeping better than usual with her in my arms, I made sure to set an alarm so that she wouldn't miss the perfect announcement of her surprise. As it goes off beside the cabin's king-sized bed, I wake immediately, looking out the window to see the dark sky starting to attempt to lighten, the sun beating against and chasing away the darkness.

Waking Dolos first, he goes to the main cabin to let the steward know that we'd like some coffee prepared. Once he's returned, we get out the clothes we packed for today, including the new outfit we got for Runa: an army green halter bikini to complement her skin, with a beige-colored outfit that the saleswoman called a cover-up.

She said that the braided-looking material was called crochet, the top is a cropped cami, and the bottom is a maxi skirt. I never knew women's clothes had so many terms.

She also gave us some cork-like sandals that she claimed completed the outfit. Obviously having no idea what we were doing, we were easy marks. Hopefully, she likes them. We bought a few other things but also planned to take her shopping on the island to ensure she had plenty to choose from for the rest of the time we were here.

By the time everything is ready, it's the perfect time to wake her. Climbing back onto the bed and lying on either side of her, we slowly start to trace the soft lines of her body while she sleeps. She makes sleepy noises, wiggles a bit, then stretches as her eyes flutter open, warming my heart and soul—Dolos' too, judging by the gooey, lovesick look on his face.

"Good morning, Darling," he whispers, leaning in for a kiss that makes her eyes roll, her lids falling heavily, lashes resting against her cheeks.

"Stop that. She'll miss it," I snap.

Her eyes fly open, looking between us, seemingly remembering she was in for a surprise before she hops right off the bed. "Miss what? Are we there?" Her excitement and smile are contagious as I feel my lips curling of their own accord. She must notice because her exhilaration melts into something that looks a lot like love, and I can only pray to the Goddess that this magnificent creature could learn to love a mess like me.

"First, get dressed." I smirk, gesturing to the outfit laid out for her. Her eyes dance over it, then volley between Dolos and me. We're dressed in outfits that are color-coordinated with Runa—also suggested by the same saleswomen—and judging by her slow appraisal of our bodies and her now beaming smile, I have to say the woman was right.

Slowly and purposefully sensual, she undresses and re-dresses, fully aware of what she's doing to us, trailing her fingers along her perfect curves, grasping her breasts as she adjusts them in the bikini top. I swear she whimpered when she stood bare before us, feeling the need coursing through her.

Dolos is practically drooling while I'm over here white-knuckling it to keep myself from touching her.

Satisfied at her ability to thoroughly torture us, we stand in front of her, both fully erect and trying to pretend we're not. She stifles a giggle before sniffing at the air, "Do I smell coffee?"

Dolos laughs, "I would say yes, but the coffee is for good girls, and now that you've been very naughty, I'm not sure." He makes a show of pouting and crossing his arms over his chest as she decides to let her laughter flow freely.

"So…you're saying you *don't* want me to be a naughty girl?" she says dramatically as she approaches him, batting her lashes and walking her fingers along his still-crossed forearms.

A shudder ripples through him as he smiles at her. "You're not playing fair—"

"Coffee," I interrupt with a pointed look at my brother, who has the decency to at least pretend to look thoroughly scolded as he takes her hand and practically drags her to the main cabin where coffee and the first part of our surprise await.

20 Runa

As they lead me out of the room to the main cabins of the plane, I see that all of the windows are covered by the standard little sliding blinds, and set up near one of the comfy little couches is a small table filled with coffee and croissants.

Dolos rushes from my side to stand directly in front of me, all giddy and animated. "But first, you have to close your eyes," he says softly with a smile on his face as Eris moves to stand beside him, offering me a small nod when my eyes meet his.

I raise a single eyebrow at them.

"It's a surprise," Eris says, his features softening.

Lowering my eyelids wordlessly, I wait. I hear the sound of the table being moved slightly, and then one of them takes me by both hands—Eris, I think, judging solely from the way his touch vibrates through me, the way it sparks just a little sharper. I'm pulled forward a few steps when I ask, "Can I open them?"

"No, no, not yet," Dolos says with pure enthusiasm in his voice. He helps me sit down and gets me settled in my seat, whispering, "Wait here."

My other senses consume me. My ears perking at the sound of the small airplane window being opened, my face moving towards the barely-there light, a smile stretching across my face. "Now can I open them?" I ask sweetly, my patience wearing thin, wanting to know what they're up to.

"Alright…now," Eris purrs.

I allow my eyelids to slowly open. The lights in the cabin have been turned down, and the men are both watching me with wonder in their eyes, waiting for me to look out the open window. When I finally allow my gaze to travel to the space they've set up for me, a loud and emotional gasp escapes me.

Our plane has lowered enough that I can see exactly where we are. Islands of lush greenery and bright pops of color, surrounded by the most beautiful turquoise waters. The sun is rising in front of my eyes, the sky alight with reds, oranges, and bright yellows.

After an undetermined amount of time visually consuming the place that I've dreamed of for so long, the place I never thought I'd get to go, I turn to them with tears welling in my eyes.

"You did all of this…for me?" I squeak.

They both smile, each taking one of my hands and leaning in to kiss me on the cheek.

"This is only the beginning, Darling," Dolos promises.

By the time the plane finishes the laps it was flying around the islands, I've finished my coffee and two croissants. We all buckle in as the overhead lights indicate that it's time to descend. My body is full of the nervous kind of excitement that makes you shiver and cold sweat.

I've never had a dream come true. I think to myself, realizing how true it is.

I had never even dared to dream about meeting my brother. I never thought it'd be possible, but mostly, I feared that if I did, I'd be putting him in danger, or worse, find out that he's just like our father.

I also never really allowed myself to dream of finding my mate because I didn't think I'd ever get to leave Khaos' pack lands.

Hawaii was the only dream I could actually have. It was something I could try to save up for and someday go on my own adventure. Now here I am, the one dream I had always dreamt of being able to do finally coming true, while the two dreams I couldn't bear myself to ever hope for, becoming a reality.

My body is thrumming with so many feelings—both physical and emotional—as the plane's wheels meet the pavement of the tarmac. A jolt of lust and something that feels a lot like love bolts through my bloodstream, causing me to wriggle in my seat, knowing now is not the time.

When we're finally able to disembark the aircraft, even the land around the airport property is stunning. We're immediately greeted by the sweetest humans. They welcome us warmly, giving each of us a fresh flower lei, one of them going as far as placing a flower in my hair.

As we move towards the awaiting car, the flower begins to fall from my hair, but Eris catches it, gingerly tucking it into my still French-braided hair so that it doesn't fall again. I smile at him with all the feelings coursing through me and reach onto my toes to kiss him.

He answers my call without a second thought, wrapping one arm around me, and pulling me tight against him. It was supposed to be a sweet, quick kiss, but it would seem I'm not the only one feeling all the things.

I open for him, and our tongues tangle together, trying to tell each other how we feel without using the words that Eris seems to avoid at all costs.

Dolos makes a sound somewhere between a break-it-up cough and a chuckle.

We stop, freezing in place, my cheeks heating with a blush I know even the Goddess herself can see. Eris leans in to kiss my forehead before resting his against mine. "There's more," he grumbles, reminding me that these two are standing here making my only real dream come true. I nod against him, and we move to get in the car together.

We've barely been in the car for ten minutes before our vehicle turns into a long and winding driveway that takes us up a decent-sized hill.

We pull up to an eye-catching and awkward style of home. The house itself looks like any other single-level family home with striking wooden siding and yellow-painted accents. What makes it intriguingly different is the spiraling outdoor staircase to the right, leading up to a large circular deck built on top of the home.

Dolos notices my analytical and confused inspection, having never seen anything like this before. "It's an observation deck, so you can look out over the property and the ocean," he explains, and my jaw drops open because that's amazing.

"I had no idea they built such things," I whisper, still in awe that not only does it exist, but out of all the properties they could have chosen for us to stay at, they chose this one.

When the guys have finally set all the luggage inside—because I'm basically not allowed to do anything myself anymore—I'm bouncing on the balls of my feet to go outside to see what I can view from the deck.

"Let's go then," Eris laughs, noticing my eagerness, gesturing towards the door leading back outside.

It's not that I don't care about the inside; it looks gorgeous as well, but I have to see more of the view.

Nearly sprinting through the door and around the house, I waste no time climbing the spiral staircase leading to the platform over the house, with the men right on my heels. Coming to a crashing halt and gasping for the second time today, I take it all in, turning in a circle with my hand over my mouth and tears in my eyes.

The view of the ocean, with a few cliffs overlooking the water's edge, spans almost half of the view from the observation deck. The water is calm today with little motion moving it, except for where it laps at the cliffs and beach.

This beach is also peculiar and not like most of the postcards and things you see or think of when imagining Hawaii. The beach is black.

"It's from the volcanoes," Eris explains shortly, seemingly reading my mind, as they continue to watch me absorbing it all.

When I've finally stopped turning, Dolos envelops me in his arms from where he now stands behind me. Not wanting to separate us in this moment, I reach for Eris'. He takes a step closer to us, letting me take his hand, while I continue to gawk at the beauty surrounding us.

The half of the view that is not the ocean and cliffs is lush and green, with palm trees sticking up all over, swaying in the warm breeze. There's a court of some sort—pickleball or tennis from the looks of it—and a comfortable-looking hot tub with one of those outdoor shower spigots just beside it.

Closing my eyes and leaning further into Dolos, I breathe it all in. The salt clinging to the breeze from the ocean's spray. The sweet smell of the vegetation native to the region. The scent of my mates mixed with it all, creating a physical memory I tuck into my heart to keep forever.

Releasing a heavy sigh of contentment, I open my eyes, still doing my best to devour every detail. That's when I notice, even from all the way up here, on top of this house, on top of a hill…I can't see any other houses.

The love and lust that had pressed down on me in the plane rages through my veins once more, and I decide I don't want to calm it this time.

Pulling Eris into me, I wrap my arms around his neck and kiss him, pushing everything I'm feeling through the kiss and our incomplete bond.

At the same time, I move my body into Dolos' body behind me, hoping he feels everything too.

"Claim me," I pant around Eris' mouth, begging my mates to make me theirs, "Please."

21
DOLOS

Watching her take in everything around us warms my soul in a way I never knew I could feel. I've never had the opportunity to do something like this to make someone I cared about this happy.

When her lips crash into Eris', I pull her into me by her hips, running my hands along her sides as they consume each other.

I'm doing my best not to grind against her, in case she's not ready. When she pants, "Claim me," into Eris' mouth, all hell breaks loose in my bloodstream and through the bond with my twin. My blood is pounding in my ears, and my wolf is pacing a trail beneath my skin.

Mentally pulling myself back together, I check on my brother, hoping he's finally over the reservations he was holding on to. *Are you ready for this?*

He surprises me when he answers, *More than anything in my existence.*

With him finally giving us the green light, I work my hands up her obnoxiously gorgeous body, just under the crochet material draped along her curves. Her breathing hitches when my fingers pull the strings of her bikini beneath the cover-up, letting the army green swim-fabric fall to the decking, and Eris lightly shoves them to the side with his foot.

Allowing my fingers to skim the skin of her torso before finally circling just around her nipple without making contact. She arches her breasts into my hands, begging me to touch her, whimpering into Eris' mouth as they remain lost in each other for a moment they both need.

Finally allowing my hand to grasp her breast, her muscles give out, and she begins to sink into our hold. "One minute, Darling," I rumble, handing her completely to Eris while I run back into the house to return with a large blanket and pillows. If we're going to be claiming her up here, she still needs to be comfortable.

Fumbling to move quickly, I arrange them so that they're covering the deck, and Eris brings her over to the softer space. Before they move to lay down, I hop up, sensually pulling her clothes from her body as my brother and I continue to kiss her bare skin, not leaving an inch unkissed. Still panting, she positions herself onto a pillow in the middle of the spread, waiting for us.

Her lust blown eyes are locked on us as we do her the favor of removing our clothes teasingly, because we know how much she loves to watch. She's practically drooling as we remove the last of our clothes in sync, our cocks bobbing free of their confines. Just the sight has her clenching her thighs together and her eyes nearly rolling back in her head.

Moving forward, I can't wait another moment to taste her. I'm on my knees and between her legs, kissing and nipping at the smooth skin on the inside of her thighs. She spreads herself for me, and I growl at the sight and scent of her glistening and ready for us.

"Dolos," she breathes.

Knowing what she wants, I slide two fingers inside her, watching her face move through the pleasure as her mouth opens, no sound coming out. Pumping my fingers slowly I watch her expressions, allowing her time to acclimate. I know when she's ready for more because she opens her eyes, lifts her head, and watches me, her mouth still open as the most beautiful sounds leave her.

Not breaking eye contact, fingers still moving rhythmically, I lean in and let my tongue graze her clit ever so lightly at first.

"Please," she begs. The sound of her needy voice going straight to my cock, making it twitch beneath me in want.

Giving her what she wants, I begin to work her bundle of nerves, alternating between lapping at it, circling it, and sucking on it, her hips lifting to meet the sensations of my hand and mouth bringing her pleasure.

Eris takes this moment to kneel beside her, massaging a full breast in each hand. She moves her arms, reaching for Eris with one hand and tangling her other in my hair, holding on for dear life. Her moans continue to send sparks of desire through me, and she has hardly even touched me yet.

Her hand that was grasping for Eris' thigh is now reaching for his length, something he wasn't letting her do…until now. When he finally lets her grasp him, his head falls back, his eyes closing as he growls. His hands move to pinch her nipples, causing her to cry out and throw her head back on the pillow. She begins to piston her hand along Eris' shaft, movements faltering as her own pleasure consumes her.

Removing my fingers, I smooth her wetness along her ass as she continues to writhe against my tongue, filling my senses completely with *her*. Inserting one finger at a time, I massage and stretch her, gliding my thumb into her sweet pussy. She begins to quake as I work her, her hand still in my hair, holding me tighter against her. When her body finally clenches around me, her cries echo around us. I smile against her, working her through the waves of her orgasm, and all I can think is that I can't wait to feel her come on my cock.

22
ERIS

Her perfect body lies on the pallet of pillows and blankets Dolos threw together, glowing in the aftermath of her first orgasm of the day. Her hand gently falls from my throbbing length, her touch igniting things within me that are so consuming I can't even put them into words.

The moment she wrapped her hand around me, I nearly lost it. The tingling of our bond dancing between us as she vocalized her pleasure beneath mine and my brother's ministrations was more than I expected, and I haven't even gotten inside of her yet.

We each lay beside her, and she immediately turns into Dolos, kissing him hard, no doubt tasting herself on his tongue as I grip her hips, rolling into her. She breaks their kiss, turning her sights on me.

Reaching up to hold her head, stroking my thumb along her jaw while I smile at her, she leans in, kissing me again, pushing me down on my back…and I let her. I'm not usually one to relinquish control, but for her, I fear there's nothing I wouldn't do.

Swinging her leg over my body, she hovers above me, running her nails across the ridges of my chest, her lips then kissing everywhere she touches as she moves down my body. "Wha—" I'm silenced with her finger against my lips.

"Shh, please let me have this first?" she asks with a pout on her lips. All I can do is nod as she touches and explores my body on her way to what she wants.

When she reaches my cock, grasping it in her hand, my hips jerk towards her, wanting more. She leans in, eyes locked on mine as she licks the tip, and I see stars. She's barely even touched me.

Gritting my teeth, I watch as she wraps her mouth around the head, languidly rolling her tongue against me. When her mouth descends, taking me further until I'm hitting the back of her throat, I wait for her to rise, but she doesn't. Instead, she continues to massage her tongue around my length, even going as far as to hollow her mouth, sucking hard, causing me to growl.

Like that's what she was waiting for, she finally rises, eyes never leaving mine as she begins to work her mouth along my length.

Not wanting to wait another second to be inside her, I sit up, pulling her gently off my dick, which makes a popping sound when it's free of her mouth.

Fuck, that was hot. My brother groans down our bond. *Not you, of course. Her.* He clarifies with a chuckle, moving in to where I'm laying Runa against a pillow between us, tracing his fingers over her hips as he lies beside her.

Lying on her back, looking between us on either side of her, she reaches out to touch each of us, wrapping her arms up to touch our faces, alternating pulling us in to kiss her as we work her body into need again. We're a mess of frantic hands and messy kisses when she releases my face, reaching down to direct my length exactly where she wants it.

"You're certain?" I breathe, my forehead resting against hers. I have to be sure.

Leaning back and staring straight into my eyes, all the way to my soul—to my wolf—she says, "I've never been more certain of anything. I…I love you, Eris. P-please, claim me." Her final words are choked with emotion, and for the first time in my life, my eyes grow glossy, my throat constricting with everything I'm feeling.

Crashing my mouth to hers, I try to make sure she can feel my love for her, but it doesn't feel like enough. "Fuck," I bite out, taking my length in my hands and moving it through her desire gathered for us, "I love you too. I fucking worship you, Precious. I'm *nothing* without you," inching inside of her as I finish my vows that still don't feel like enough.

"Oh…Goddess," she inhales as I fill her, stretching her slowly, her warmth consuming me.

Allowing her a moment to adjust, I slowly roll her clit beneath my thumb, allowing her to relax around me. "Breathe, baby," I purr when I realize she seems to be holding her breath. When she exhales dramatically, once again panting, water is still lining her eyes. I lean in to kiss away a stray tear that breaks free. "I've got you. Are you okay?"

She nods, wriggling her hips, looking down at where we're joined, my knot resting just outside her entrance, "Yes. I'm ready," she rasps. I begin to slowly roll my hips, feeling every inch of her walls clinging to me as I pull out to the tip and all the way back in, savoring every fucking inch.

Once her muscles are completely relaxed, I turn us, still connected, so that we're lying on our sides. Her eyebrows raise in silent question just before Dolos rolls as well, his chest now pressing against her back.

23 Runa

I'm so fucking full, and we've barely even began.

I'm not a virgin by any means, but as a different way to remain faithful to my mate—well, mates—I only ever had human men before. While they got the job done enough to take the edge off, it was nothing like this all-consuming feeling.

I have never been as stretched as I am now, and I still have to take Dolos. The thought has my eyes rolling back in my head while Eris rolls himself into me again and again.

With Dolos now pressed against my back, I am completely wrapped in the warmth of them. I feel Dolos move, slightly leaning away from me. When he rolls back into me, Eris grunts, reaching for my leg, lifting it, and wrapping it around his hip as he rocks into me again, reaching a place inside of me I hadn't even known existed. I don't even try to contain the sounds leaving my mouth, vocalizing everything I'm feeling in this space where words aren't as needed.

Dolos' hand trails down my spine, all the way between my cheeks, and begins to massage my other hole, coating me in the lubricant he must have been reaching for. A hoarse cry leaves me at all the sensations flying through me when he plunges two fingers into me. Eris stills deep inside of me, allowing Dolos to work my muscles, stretching me to allow me to take him.

"Yes, yes, yes," I chant as I try to breathe. "Eris," I plead, not knowing exactly what I even want, but he does. He moves his hand to rub circles around my clit as they both pull out of me at once, leaving me feeling empty…but for only a second.

They're both positioned at my entrances, waiting for me. My nerves consume me, and I try to hold in the shiver of need that courses through me, my wolf just under my skin, whining for her mates to claim her.

Dolos works the tip of his cock inside of my ass slowly, gently. The sting of stretch grows as I take him in a way I've never had anyone. "Shit," I breathe heavily, and he stops. While he remains still, my body trying to decide what to do with the new intrusion, Eris slides back inside of me, sending me arching into Dolos.

We all curse at once from the pleasure washing over us. Eris rocks into me in painfully slow strokes, gently rubbing my clit, my body finally starting to relax around Dolos. I tilt my head back, laying it on Dolos' shoulder. He nibbles my ear, reaching around my body to pluck at my nipple, whispering how much of a good girl I am.

He reaches behind himself again, returning and adding more lube to his shaft, massaging my tight ring of muscles, and pushing himself further into me. I scream as a spontaneous orgasm rushes through my body without warning, both men using their hands to work my body through the aftershocks.

But it's not enough. It's still not enough. "Keep going," I beg, trying to move my body between them. I need their knots. I need their marks. I need to claim them.

Dolos moves first, almost fully seating himself inside me finally, my breath coming quickly as I try to breathe around being so full of both of them. When I feel his knot press against me, Eris returns to his rhythm, rocking into me. I'm drowning in pleasure, wave after wave rolling through me. I feel frantic with the need to claim them, my mind no longer able to make sense of what I'm feeling.

Dolos slowly starts working my ass, and I swear, there is electricity flying through my veins, lighting up every sensitive nerve ending, answering the call of my mates.

"Come for us," Eris snarls, once again circling my clit while they both drive into me at their own speeds. Words are lost to me, I couldn't string together a coherent thought if I tried, so I focus on everything I'm feeling at once. Their movements become stuttered; knowing they're close has me on the precipice of something I know I'll never recover from.

"Keep breathing, Darling," Dolos rumbles through gritted teeth, shoving his knot inside of me as I combust through an orgasm that makes the edge of my vision blur white.

Only to be immediately followed by Eris' knot slamming inside of me, detonating another orgasm I was not prepared for, peppering my vision with black dancing flickers. They roar their release together, filling me so completely as their knots begin to swell, and I scream through a third orgasm that feels like I might be dying of pleasure and love.

I feel one of them gathering my hair in their hands just before they both lick either side of my neck. *Oh, fuck. This is it. Yes, yes, YES!*

Their teeth sink into my neck, and I black out for a instant from the sheer intensity of it all.

We all come again, them spilling into me further, my body locking even harder around their swollen knots. They retract their fangs, licking the wounds, and while I'm still conscious, I lean forward, licking the right side of Eris' neck, before allowing my teeth to elongate and claiming him, as he comes inside me again, roaring as our bond snaps into place, his love and pleasure filling me so suddenly, tears trickle down my cheeks.

Retracting my fangs and awkwardly turning my body as best as I can locked between my mates, I lick the left side of Dolos' neck before claiming him as well, his body reacting the same way as Eris', spilling inside of me. His voice thunders around us, our bond snapping into place, and just before I remove my fangs, a strange feeling washes over me that feels like both bonds connecting and creating one large bond.

I'm completely overwhelmed with the love, worry, care, wonder, adoration, and concern from my mates, washing over me through our bond.

Are you okay? Eris' worried voice finds me first, and I try to open my eyes to look at him, but I don't have any energy left to do even that.

"Mmhmm," I mumble happily, fighting the sleep threatening to pull me under.

I feel their bodies wrap around me, their knots still swollen inside of me.

Perfect, I'm absolutely perfect, I tell them both through our bond before I allow the sleepiness to drag me into the blissful darkness.

24
DOLOS

Keeping my eyes closed, I bask in the warmth of my mate's soft skin against mine, the calmness of her aura while she sleeps slowly trickling down our mate bond, intertwined with my brother's strangely calm energy—he's usually wound tighter than a drum.

I've been awake for a while, but I haven't even had the desire to open my eyes. If I open them, I'll be fully awake, and my emotions could wake them.

Judging by the lack of blazing sun on my skin, I'd wager we managed to sleep the entire day away. Though, that does mean we laid in the island's sun all day long—naked—and if we weren't werewolves, we'd likely have third-degree burns.

While I'm not exactly upset about sleeping the day away—we all clearly needed the rest—I do hope Runa isn't disappointed by missing out on her entire first day in Hawaii.

As a cool, sweet breeze rolls against our skin, I replay the look of wonder on her face as she took in our vacation home, then sprinted up the stairs to the deck. I remind myself that we need to spend more time on the rooftop at home, maybe even finally building a cabin on the packlands with a similar observation deck overlooking the massive lake.

Eris and I hadn't elected to build our own home on the property because we were always just wherever Roman and the rest of our tightly-knit group were. We'd all just chosen to stay in the Alpha's cabin—before Leera came along anyways. I wouldn't dare interrupt them now.

Finally opening my eyes, the air is knocked from my lungs at the view of my slumbering mate lying on her back between us, illuminated only by the bright light of the moon. Both of her shoulders are adorned with nearly matching mate marks. My chest constricts at the sight before me.

The patterns shockingly resemble waves of the ocean and are practically identical, but if you look close enough, you can easily tell them apart. The pale, almost-white lines look like long-healed scars against her golden skin. Eris' mark is made of jagged and barbed lines, making the waves look angry, as though you're encountering a storm at sea, while the lines of my mark are smooth, like a calm day at the beach with soft, rolling waves.

My fingers itch to trace the lines across her skin, and to see the marks that my brother and I have, but I still, trying not to move. I'm surprised my reaction to the marks hasn't already woken them, but I can't contain the way my heart soars at the sight of everything before me.

My thoughts are suddenly drawn to a tickling feeling on my leg. My eyes instinctually slide to my mate and twin, but they are both still very much asleep. Cautiously turning my head, I'm unable to contain myself when I yelp and jump from where I was lying because there is a freaking gecko crawling up my leg.

Runa startles awake like the cute, main character in a movie, while Eris springs into action, taking his battle stance with fists raised, ready to take on a monster—still completely naked, mind you.

"Uh…sorry," I chuckle, "gecko." I finish, shrugging my shoulder in embarrassment.

As Runa's eyes focus, I can physically see her processing my words before she bursts into laughter. She doesn't just laugh. She laughs so hard she's clutching her middle, doubling over, and wheezing with tears escaping her eyes.

"Yes, yes, hilarious," I mock-scold with a smile while she tries to get herself together, earning me a pillow thrown at my head from Eris, who has calmed and now sits next to Runa.

When she can finally breathe and wipes the last of her happy tears from her face, she looks to me and is about to say something when she stills, mouth hanging open on the words she was about to say. Her eyes fill with new tears, but they're not humorous or sad; I can feel the love rushing through our bond like a raging river.

Our marks, I think to myself just as she reaches out to touch mine. The action bringing my cock to attention, a shiver rolling through my limbs.

Ignoring the desire trying to take over this moment, I'm finally able to see Eris' marks and part of mine. From what I can see, they are identical. Two sets of waves. The ones on each side of Runa's neck. We each have our own set of waves on our shoulder where she marked us. Her head moves back and forth, looking between our marks before noticing her own on either side of her neck.

"They're perfect," she squeaks, reaching for us.

We simultaneously lean into her, our foreheads resting on either side of her face; all of our eyes close as we are consumed by the moment. *You're perfect,* Eris promises through our bond, I allow my eyes to open, finding her face lit up with his words and being able to communicate through our bond.

Leaning forward, I pepper kisses along her collarbone, teasing the skin close to her new mark. *How are you feeling?* I ask before I get her all wound up. It's the first time she's taken two men at once—before you consider our knots. I don't want to take her again if she's still sore.

She wriggles where she sits, checking herself. *I'm perfect,* she answers cheekily. *Must have healed all up while we slept; I expected to at least be a little sore…* Her face stills in realization. "We slept all day?" she says in a way that makes it sound more like a question, but I think she meant it as a statement.

Nodding, I answer cautiously, hoping again that she's not upset to have missed her first day of vacation. "It would appear so. That may be why you're feeling okay."

Springing from where she was settled between us, she stands over us and starts gathering clothes. She collects mine first, throws them at me, and repeats the process with Eris' clothes before she begins pulling her own over her body I was hoping to taste more of.

"Get dressed, boys; you're taking me to the beach," she beams, and there's no way either of us could say no if we had wanted to.

25
ERIS

Runa's excitement is a living, bubbling thing cascading through our bond, mixing with the love and wonder my brother has, feeling how happy she is to see the ocean. She didn't want to drive the short distance to the private beach that's part of the property we've rented, so the three of us are walking hand-in-hand along the lush, green pathway. Runa walks between us, holding each of our hands, swinging them back and forth with the steps she takes, carrying us closer and closer to making her dream come true.

The smell and taste of salt, of the ocean, grows heavier with every step we take; the moonlight glowing around us in the crisp night air as the sound of the water lapping at the shore reaches us. At the sound, Runa perks up even further, glancing at each of us before she takes off, sprinting the final distance of the path.

Breaking through the green curtain of palm and monstera leaves that open to the private cove, Runa's breath catches. The cove is even more magnificent than the pictures Dolos and I had seen. It was one of the main reasons we picked this house, though I'm pleased with how enamored our mate was with the observation deck.

The beach is made up of black sand from the volcanic activity on the islands. The Goddess must have known we'd be here because the moon currently sets in the sky perfectly centered by the cliffs surrounding us. The water steadily rolls against the shore, creating the whispering sounds humans pay to listen to while they sleep.

I'm watching Runa take in the scene before us, and Dolos, who is also watching her. Her forehead creases and her eyebrows scrunch in concentration before she suddenly slams her hands over her mouth, staring at us with wide, glossy eyes. *Do you see that?!* she whisper-squeals through our bond, causing me to chuckle because we're the only two that can hear her.

Yes, Precious, the cove is beautiful, but it has nothing on you, I purr, earning a snort from Dolos. *Why are you whisper-shouting at us?*

Her hands fall from her face, her jaw dropping. *How have you not noticed them?* she asks in the same aggravated undertone, gesturing towards the beach in front of us.

Dolos and I obediently redirect our attention to the beach, and at first, I don't know what she's on about. As I stare at the black sand beach, looking for what she's talking about, I notice…well that doesn't make sense. The sand looks like it's moving. Returning our attention to our mate, Dolos blurts out loud, "Why is the sand moving?"

Runa obnoxiously shushes him, being much louder than he was in her attempt to keep him quiet before elaborating, *The sand isn't moving! Look closer. Focus on one spot of movement near you,* she instructs us, her voice full of awe.

Concentrating on one of the moving areas only a couple of feet from where we stand, I see what has her body thrumming in a mixture of protectiveness, happiness, and love.

Crawling out of and across most of the sand covering the beach are baby sea turtles crawling for the ocean.

Sending thanks to the Goddess for making this even more special for our mate, I step behind Runa, carefully watching my steps, and wrap my arms around her. She leans into me, resting her hands on my arms, and fuck, I once again find myself feeling things I've never felt before. Things that are inappropriate to be thinking already. We just claimed her. But her protective instinct over these creatures has me thinking about little creatures we might have some day.

Our moment isn't broken, but it does change, because I'm reminded that this bond is not just Runa's and mine. It is also Dolos', and he makes it known by pushing me slightly to the side, sliding in behind her, and also wrapping his arm around her, her body now leaning into both of ours as we watch the tiny animal skitter across the sand.

We continue to watch Runa, completely transfixed by what's happening, when we feel her begin to worry, the bitter feeling filling our senses as it floods our bond.

"What's wrong, Darling?" Dolos asks quietly as not to feel her wrath by being too loud again.

Her eyes dart around the cove, wringing her hands in front of her. Every muscle in her body looks coiled to spring into action at the drop of whatever she's panicked over. "We're not the only ones that have noticed the babies."

The way she says babies has that thing I was feeling, twitching deep within me. *It's not the time to explore this*, I remind my wolf who I've decided to blame for reacting this way.

When her words finally register, I notice what she sees.

There are island predators closing in from the sky and the sand. Birds and crabs are beginning to gather, watching the hatchlings make their way toward the ocean, following the light of the moon.

A crab jerks towards one of the baby sea turtles, and Runa's muscles fire a fraction of a second later, batting the crab across the sand and away from the hatchling it was within reach of. "Help me!" she cries, darting towards a bird that landed next to another turtle. She turns and faces us with a fierceness I haven't seen her wear, her eyes full of a wild fury, and it takes a conscious effort not to get hard at the sight.

"What do you expect us to do? Run all over the beach all night while they hatch?" Dolos asks, totally stunned by her sudden need to protect the tiny beings.

I'm smart enough to keep my mouth shut based on the look on her face. She turns to him and crosses her arms with a huff, eyes still scanning the beach for dangers. "That's exactly what I'm asking you to do. Is there a problem with that?" she bites.

Barking out a laugh, I shoo away a bird while Dolos' jaw hangs open at being scolded by our mate. Her sheer determination hits me square in the chest through our bond, and I know she means business. No matter why it means so much to her, we'll make sure all of them make it safely to the ocean. After that, their survival is on them.

26
Runa

Just as the sun begins to rise on our second day in Hawaii, we usher the last baby turtle to the ocean, protecting it from anything that might want to eat it, all of us collapsing into a pile on the beach.

Nuzzling into Eris, I mumble, "Thank you for helping me," as I reach for Dolos with my hand. "Both of you."

They both bark a small laugh, and Eris responds, "You didn't give us much of a choice." He kisses the top of my head. "You're welcome. But… why was that so important to you, Precious?"

At first, I realize I didn't understand either, so I take a minute to arrange my thoughts before I tell them, "They're just babies. They had no one to protect them while others were trying to kill them…I guess I felt a connection to them. I needed to make sure they were okay."

The realization weighs heavy on all of us that had my mother not fought so hard for my life, I wouldn't be here. Would the Goddess have given me another chance within this same lifetime, or would my mates have spent their existences alone?

Our bond is a mess of heavy feelings when Dolos draws me into him, his lips claiming mine in a hungry kiss. A kiss that feels like he's showing himself and his wolf that I'm here and I'm safe with them.

While Dolos devours my mouth, Eris leans in, tracing my body lightly with his fingertips before he slides the fabric of my halter bikini off my breast, lapping at it and kissing me through my crochet cover-up, with the same fervor as Dolos takes my mouth.

My body sparks and tingles under their touch, moaning into Dolos' mouth as our love, desire, and melancholy blend together through our bond. Tears prick my eyes at the gravity of what could have been, knowing they could have been left alone without their mate. Of all the other bonds broken by my father's sins.

Not having the patience for foreplay and also not wanting sand in all of my everything, I beg my mates through our bond, not wanting to stop kissing and touching them, *I need you both. Now. Stand up, take me, please.*

In a strong gracefulness I attribute to their hockey careers, they stand as one, lifting me as if I weigh nothing. The sunrise glows over us as they hold onto me. Dolos' arms wrapped under my knees, my body between them, leaning into Eris' warmth behind me. They each elongate a claw, snapping my brand-new bikini off my body. *I hadn't even gotten to swim in that,* I whine.

Their laughter rumbles through me. *We'll buy you as many as you want, Darling,* Dolos tells me with amusement.

Their hands and mouths are everywhere, mine just trying to keep up, trying to pull their trunks down enough to free them for me. When my fumbling fingers are able to release them, one at a time, their groans make me burn brighter.

Eris moves first, running the head and shaft of his length through my gathering desire, coating himself in me, rubbing his head against my clit. My head falls back onto his shoulder, and he sucks on his mate mark on my neck, nearly making me come from the sensations alone.

As Dolos begins to massage my clit now with the head of his shaft, Eris sets himself at my rear entrance, sending sparks of pleasure, burning my bloodstream. The moan that leaves me would be embarrassing if I didn't feel so good right now. With his head inside my tight ring of muscles, he doesn't move as Dolos guides himself to my wet center.

He slides himself inside of me, and while he does, Eris matches his movements. I'm gasping for air as they fill me completely, consuming my every sense with *them*. I don't think I'll ever get used to the fullness or how right it feels for the three of us to be one in like this.

Turning my head to kiss Eris, Dolos then takes my breast in his mouth just before he begins to lift me, retracting their dicks from my body before slamming me back down on them, my cries echoing through the cove.

We continue to move through the warm heat of the morning sun, our bodies coated in dew and sweat, the swells of pleasure growing until their movements become erratic. They both bite down on my new mate marks, and I'm capsized by my orgasm. My body shakes and trembles as they come with me.

With one final hard thrust, they give me their knots, and I cry out as the pleasure explodes through my veins and forces me through another orgasm, my muscles quaking as they swell inside of me, locking the three of us together.

My head falls forward onto Dolos' chest, all of us panting and heaving for oxygen. I don't know how they're still standing—I would have crumpled into a pile of satisfaction—but they hold me strong, their muscles not showing any sign of strain at holding my limp body between them.

I love you both so fucking much, I promise through our bond. Both of them lean in to kiss me on my head.

We love you more, Eris vows.

What he said, Dolos adds.

27
DOLOS

After carrying Runa back to the house, we took her to the shower, washed every inch of her perfect golden skin, claimed her again, and then she washed us. The mundane actions filling me with a peace I've never known. This is our life. She's ours. Forever.

Before we arrived, we had paid for the kitchen to be fully stocked with fresh food. Setting her in a bamboo barstool at the small breakfast bar, we make our way into the kitchen and work in tandem to make a large breakfast spread with an obnoxious amount of fresh fruit. She dives into the pineapple first, telling us it's her favorite fruit, another piece of information about our mate to commit to memory.

Pineapple juice dribbles down her chin, and it takes all my strength not to dive across the counter, lick it up, and claim her again, but I can't. We have plans for our sweet mate today, and *that* will have to wait until later this evening before we can be inside her again.

When we finally make it out of the house, all of us are wound a little tight from trying to keep our hands to ourselves. Wishing we could have had more days in paradise so we weren't rushed to make all of her dreams come true. We head back out into the bright sunlight beaming over the islands on our way to the day's first excursion.

She peppers us with questions, trying to get us to spill our secrets, and we somehow manage to keep a lid on them until we arrive. There are already people everywhere, but the owner of our vacation home raved about the large island market that would be buzzing with activity. Her head remains on a swivel, following the sights and sounds all around us, her excitement palpable in the warm air.

Lined up and down the long Main Street are vendors of all kinds, the early morning light streaming between the booths. There are little food trucks and booths with scents of roasted meats and sweet treats fogging the air. There are seamstresses and crafters selling handmade clothes, jewelry, art, souvenirs, and more, all wearing warm, easy smiles as they watch patrons move along the road, currently closed off to traffic.

Even though we ate not long ago, the scent of pineapple-roasted meat draws her in first, and I'm definitely not complaining—it smells amazing. The decadence of the aroma alone makes my mouth water. Eris orders each of us a grilled kebab that is heavily loaded with chicken, onion, peppers, and pineapple.

Runa eagerly takes a bite, moaning her enjoyment, my brother and I freezing as we absorb the sound, a few other men eyeing our beautiful mate, causing me to growl. "Maybe save those sounds for just the three of us," I suggest roughly.

She giggles.

Brat.

Moving along, she stops and checks out booths full of mugs, clothing, trinkets, and every kind of souvenir you could imagine. She buys a few handmade dresses and a magnet, but she still seems to be searching for something as her eyes scan every inch of each vendor's booth, looking irritated when she doesn't find what she deems to be the perfect treasure.

We're about to leave when she pulls on my arm, bolting out of our grasp, and rushes to a tiny booth that's actually just a table set up with a few very eclectic things adorned on it. Behind it sits the sweetest little old woman, her eyes crinkling with a wide smile she grants Runa as she approaches.

Scanning the table, I see what made her so happy. I wasn't even aware what she was looking for, but it all makes sense now. Sea turtles. The table is covered in sea turtles of all kinds. Wood carvings, handmade jewelry, keychains, postcards, stickers—you name it.

Eris smiles with his hands in his pockets as he watches her take it all in. In a flash, it looks as though something catches his eye. He moves to the table, picking up something beaded without her noticing, too engulfed in her exploration of the other items on the surface. Discreetly, he shows me the turquoise beads making up a small bracelet. *What's so special about that?* I ask.

He rolls his eyes at me in the way that tells me he thinks I'm completely dense. *Only that the beads are our favorite color, and,* he turns the bracelet, and it definitely makes sense. There's a turtle bead, also carved out of turquoise.

He moves quickly and quietly to purchase it without her noticing. When he turns to give it to her, she's holding up one that matches it perfectly, except the one in her hand is made of pink turquoise. "I want to get this for Leera." She smiles, beaming really, at the gift she's chosen for our Luna and basically her sister-in-law…

Wait, does that make her our sister-in-law now too? I think to myself. I'll inquire about that later.

Eris' mouth stretches into a grin so big I worry his recently serious face might crack when he says, "Of course, Precious, but we got this one for you," he says as he presents her with the bracelet matching the one in her hand.

She gasps, her eyes once again filling with happy tears, "You bought this for me?" She looks to me for confirmation, like she doesn't believe it, so I nod to her with a smile.

Without hesitation she launches herself at my twin, one arm extended to pull me in for a group hug, the older woman smiling as she takes us in.

"I'm so lucky to have you two." She mumbles emotionally into his shirt.

Shaking my head, using my thumb and finger to pull her chin back so she's facing me, I say, "We're the lucky ones, Darling. Don't you ever forget it," I tell her, a bit more seriously than I intended.

Eris takes her hand in his, slipping the bracelet onto her slender wrist, the turquoise beads popping beautifully off her skin. She watches with tears still in her eyes, turning her wrist every which way to admire her new treasure. It isn't much, but it makes her happier than I've ever seen, and that's all that matters…and an idea takes form.

28
ERIS

After taking all of our purchases back to the house, Dolos mumbles something about needing to take care of something and swears he'll be back in time for our evening plans. Runa again tries to get answers from me, but if I wasn't telling her our measly surprises until now, there's no way in hell I'm telling her this one.

Once she gives up, her and I get changed into fresh swim clothes, and I pack a cooler to take down to the cove, intent on spending the day on the beach with my mate.

She's fucking glowing in her dark turquoise bikini. I don't understand how the top stays up because it doesn't have straps holding it up. It's banded across her chest, the fabric looking as though it twists between her perfect breasts. The bottom piece is a scrap of material that I wouldn't have chosen if we were in a public setting, since gouging people's eyes out is frowned upon among humans.

Taking her hand in mine, collecting all of our beach things with the other, we walk out the door and down to the cove.

With the sun now high in the sky, the black sand is much hotter than it was overnight, but she doesn't seem to mind at all, kicking off her flimsy foam sandals and bolting towards the water.

She crashes into the ocean, not stopping, water splashing everywhere. She's radiant in unbridled joy as it swells through our bond, overtaking me completely. I'm smiling like the fool I once portrayed, but the gesture has never been more real. Turning from her, I set us up a little space with the sand blanket, cooler, and beach chairs under a straggling palm tree.

Satisfied with my work, I turn back to the ocean, unable to immediately see Runa, and panic begins to set in, my head thrashing in every direction, trying to find her. Her torso comes exploding out of the water, her eyes telling me she could feel my terror through our bond. *I'm here, Eris. I'm okay.* She offers me a small, guilty smile for worrying me.

I rush towards her.

The second she's in my arms, the ocean surrounding us, I can't keep my lips from hers. She meets my tongue without hesitation, letting our bodies smooth the concern that had tried to demolish me. She rocks her body against me, my hands gripping the flawless curves of her ass as the overwhelming need to take her barrels through me, my cock fully on board with the thought.

She pulls back, her bright green eyes watching me, reading me. Removing her hands from around my neck, she reaches behind her own body, freeing her breasts, allowing them to barely graze the water. Bringing one hand up to pinch her pert, rosy nipple. She moans, her head falling back, and I can't stop myself from leaning forward and sucking on my mark on her skin.

Well, that's one way to keep her distracted from what I'm doing. Dolos' voice is filled with humor as he must be feeling everything through our bond.

My snickering out loud causes her to lift her head, a single dark eyebrow raised in question. "Dolos can feel us. Let's give him a show, shall we?" I offer.

Her eyes light up, burning with mischief and the same desire I'm feeling.

"Absolutely," she groans, reaching down to pull the tiny strings on the hips of her bikini bottoms. I pull each hand away to collect the garment, tossing it to the shoreline where the top already lies in the sand.

She then reaches between us, lining me up with her entrance. I've barely pressed inside her when she grips my shoulders and slams her hips down, impaling herself on me, causing us both to moan.

She rides me hard, waves lapping around us. Reaching one of my hands around her, I tease her rear entrance with my finger, circling the tight ring of muscles. "Oh, fuck…yes…please," she begs as she continues to take what she needs from me.

With one finger inside her ass, her muscles begin to clench. "Not yet, Precious," I purr. The other hand, not pleasuring her backside, moves to her shoulder, stopping her movements, only my finger still working her body.

Her eyes flash to mine. "What? Why?" she barks, her voice frustrated from stalling her release.

Leaning in closer, I lick the column of her neck. "Because"—I nip at her mark—"if I draw it out, you'll come even harder," I inform her, as she whimpers.

Once she's calmed enough that her muscles are no longer clenching or quaking as they had begun to do, I release her shoulder. "Ride me slow. Make it last," I challenge her.

Her face is determined as she slowly starts rolling her hips again, my finger still in her ass, matching her movements. Her eyes are locked on mine as we pant together. "Good-fucking-girl. Nice and slow," I praise her. "When you feel it rising, try to relax. Don't focus on it," I coach her, edging her towards a more intense orgasm.

"Ohhh…oh, shit…Eris," she whines, and I take that as my cue.

No longer able to stave off my own quickly approaching climax, I begin to slam into her, adding another finger to her ass and pumping into her with the same rhythm as my hips.

Her body begins to tighten around me, so I lean forward and bite down hard on her mark at the same moment I slam my knot inside of her. She screams her release so hard, two birds take flight, and I worry that she'll be hoarse later, but those thoughts become obsolete as my climax shoots through me, pumping inside of her.

She rests her head on my shoulder as she heaves, and as soon as I've recovered from my own release, I walk our still-locked bodies to the shore, not stopping to gather her bikini from the sand.

As gently as I can, I lower myself into one of the beach chairs, her body still limply resting against mine. Stretching my legs out in front of me, I pop open the cooler to grab two bottles of water. Chugging mine and setting hers beside her for when she's ready.

Finally raising her torso, she once again latches her eyes to mine as she chugs her water, leans over to set it beside her, and rises with an ornery as hell smile on her face. "You're right, that was amazing." She jerks her hips, my previously softening knot hardening once more.

"Fuck, woman," I yelp in sensitive surprise.

She trails her fingers down my abdomen. "I want another one," she whispers as she slams her body down hard, crying out at the sensations of fucking herself on my very swollen cock.

She rides me again, this time like a woman obsessed, and damn if I'm going to stop her. Running my hands up her legs, I grip her ass. Moving my hands back to the front of her, I latch onto her breasts as they bounce in front of me.

Yes, yes, yes, she chants through our bond, and I swear, I heard Dolos groaning with us.

When her body once again tightens, I meet her, thrust for thrust, rutting up into her, and she slams herself down while I continue to pinch the tips of her nipples with both hands.

All of a sudden, she's screaming her release, her body locking around mine, and this time she leans forward, biting my bite mark, resulting in me roaring another release with her.

When we both finally come down from the high, we spend another solid hour on the beach, basking in nature—and each other—before heading back to the vacation home to get ready for this evening's festivities.

29
Runa

I nearly stab myself in the eye with my mascara wand when Dolos bangs into the house, an irritated sort of desire flooding our bond, causing me to smirk while I try to pretend I'm not affected by his need for me.

"Do you two know how absolutely awful it is to get hard and moan in the middle of a j—" he rants until Eris cuts him off with a shot to the gut judging by the "oomph" sound that left him.

"Oh, don't be such a baby," he scoffs, unimpressed by his twin's outburst, a playful look of warning on his face.

Dolos doesn't say anything else, but I hear him stomping towards the bathroom. Stomping towards me. I turn to smile at him as he reaches the doorway, tossing my make-up in my travel case on the counter, but he doesn't stop and goof around like I expected. Instead, he presses himself against my back, his face in my neck as he inhales deeply, grinding against my backside.

Moving my chin up so I'm looking at the two of us in the mirror, his eyes meet mine, his face breaking into a breathtakingly handsome smile, all seriousness gone now that we're together. "That was awfully naughty of you, you know." He pouts dramatically, making me giggle.

"Are you saying if the tables were turned, you wouldn't have taken me? You would have made me wait?" I pout dramatically back. *Two can play at that game.*

He looks to the ceiling as he groans, mulling over my words. "I suppose you're right," he adds, and I think that's all, but he deftly flips up the back of the dress that Eris gave me to wear tonight. It's a flowy and tiered white maxi dress with the front looking as though it crosses over my breast into a thin halter, with a sliver of my abdomen showing.

"Dolos!" I admonish, "What are you doing?" I giggle, trying to swat at his hands, but I know what he's doing. I can feel his hard length pulsing against me. I can feel his desire washing over me, his scent growing musky in the small space, my eyes nearly rolling as my need grows along with his, my thighs growing slick with anticipation.

He lands a loud slap on my ass. "And no panties, what a wicked little mate you are," he purrs against my neck, running the head of his cock through my folds.

"We don't have time for this!" Eris hollers from somewhere in the house, his footsteps moving towards us as he no doubt is feeling something very similar to what Dolos endured earlier.

Leaning back into him, encouraging him to take me, I whine, "Better make it quick then. I'd like to come before we leave," I finish with a wink, the stupid gorgeous man behind me growling as he fills me slowly, his face carved with pleasure in the mirror.

Bracing my hands on the counter, he wastes no time in picking up the pace, my breasts bouncing hard enough I wonder if they'll escape my dress. I try to keep my eyes open so that I can watch us in the mirror, but when Eris stands in the doorway, unzipping his shorts and stroking himself while his twin takes me, overwhelms me and my eyes close as my head falls back, gasping for oxygen.

Sliding his hand from my hips to my center, Dolos massages my clit, groaning in my ear, "Come with me, Darling." And fuck if I could stop myself when he says things like that.

My body detonates and my legs give out. I lean my torso on the cool counter, breaths still heaving, stars dancing behind my eyelids as my mates come at the same time. Dolos slaps me hard on the ass as he works his knot into me, another orgasm tearing through my body, short-circuiting my brain momentarily.

Once I've caught my breath, Dolos still locked inside of me, I smile at my mates. Eris moves to clean himself, then leaves the room, bringing back his brother's clothes for the night and a lacy thong for me. "As much as I'd love for you to never wear underwear, I don't trust myself with you in public without them."

When Dolos is able to remove himself from my core, he does so gently, stopping me from moving as I try to rise. He turns on the faucet and snatches a clean washcloth from the towel rack in the corner, cleaning me with care.

Adjusting myself while I check my hair and make-up, I smile to myself, happier than I've ever been in my entire life.

It takes us about an hour and a half to drive across The Big Island to get to wherever we're going. As sunset nears, we drive along the ocean for a minute, and I notice the beaches are no longer black, the sand returning to the more traditional Hawaiian view.

Eris pulls the car into a large resort's parking lot, his right hand keeping a firm hold on my thigh, Dolos squirming with enthusiasm in the back seat, his smile taking over his face.

Glancing out the windows, I still can't quite see what we're here for, but I notice a glow of lights on the far side of the property near the beach.

My body is alight with jittery excitement as Dolos beats Eris to open my door, offering me his hand to hold as they lead me towards the beach.

I have to verbally coach myself through not asking twenty more times where we're going or what we're doing as we make the trek across the parking lot.

When we're close enough to see down to the beach, the first thing I notice is the stage and all the tiki torches sending firelight into the air around us, and my brain catches up. "A luau?" I blurt, thrilled to experience something so magical in its own way.

As we approach the hostess stand, Eris moves ahead of us, giving his name for our reservation. The beautiful young woman looks over us curiously, her cheeks pinkening at either the sight of my mates or the fact that I'm with both of them. *Most humans don't get it,* Dolos snickers through our bond, stealing the edge of embarrassment that had attempted to shadow me.

We're led to our seats right in front of the stage and given stunning leis made of shells. Dolos pulls my chair out for me as we wait for our waitress.

After she explains the buffet and scurries away with our drink orders, we make our way towards the massive rows of food.

I don't even know where to start. There's so much delicious food available, and I want to try it all. On the cold bar, there's traditional salad, sweet potato macaroni salad, some kind of poi, pineapple, and coconut rolls. I grab some of everything but the poi, which oddly enough looks like the infamous "gray stuff" in that children's movie Leera made me watch.

The boys go full carnivore, loading their plates with the teriyaki beef, Kailua pork and cabbage, and steamed fresh fish, neither one of them grabbing any vegetables that aren't mixed with the meat. Don't get me wrong, I grab some of everything, but I grab some grilled veggies and rice to balance it all.

When we get back to our table, our Mai Tais await, condensation already gathering on the glasses. We settle in and taste everything. I moan at the flavors overwhelming my senses. Eris' eyes snap to mine, Dolos adjusts himself without shame, and I smother a snicker to keep myself from laughing out loud with a mouth full of food.

"Precious, I'm really going to have to insist that you refrain from *that,* if at all possible," he begins. *Killing human men for their reactions to you is frowned upon.*

Thankfully, I'd finished chewing my food by the time he blurted that out because a choked laugh did escape me this time. *That's a little dramatic, don't we think?*

They both stare at me seriously, shaking their heads no, and I can't help but laugh again. *Okay, okay, I'm sorry. Down, boys.* I smile at them, and they seem to relax…for now, at least.

When we've cleared our plates, we return to the buffet for dessert. Because I'm a glutton for punishment, and even though my tongue is already burning from all the pineapple, I grab another pile. Adding Hawaiian Haupia pudding, coconut cake, and fresh papaya to my plate. I make my way back to the table just as the sun begins to set and the show begins.

With the sun fully set over the legendary shores of the bay, we're immersed in captivating stories from the South Pacific through mesmerizing songs, dances, and tales. You can see the people's love for their legends and traditions on their faces. It's beautifully devastating. We clap and cheer and shout along with the intimate crowd.

As the evening comes to a close, the music swells and expands with a thundering intensity. It fills my body, my every pore. Closing my eyes and basking in everything surrounding me, gasps around me cause me to jerk my eyelids up, and suddenly, there are fire dancers on the stage.

Their movements are powerful and primal, owning the space around them. The fire is stunning, the dancers are entrancing, but the music… the music is intoxicating, and it's not the Mai Tais. The beating of the drums and the chants of their people swelling a need within me, making me feel like I'm on fire myself.

30
ERIS

My wolf howls beneath my skin. I can feel my body prickling, my pupils dilating. Freezing in my seat, I chance a glance at my twin, who returns the same look on his face that I feel on my own.

Shit, he groans to me through our bond.

We rise slowly, trying not to scramble and draw attention from the humans surrounding us. I cautiously extend my hand to Runa, hoping she accepts it without a stubborn fuss.

Her hooded gaze meets mine, pupils totally blown as she begins to wriggle in her seat. Her scent has become so strong that I don't feel like I'm getting any oxygen. My eyes frantically take in our surroundings, making sure there aren't any other shifters in the vicinity. The last thing we need is other males to catch her scent right now. Mated or not, you never know if there are other assholes out there.

"Is it time to go?" she nearly pants, confusion crinkling her brow. She's so fucking spectacular, staring at me with her green gaze, clouded with her growing lust.

Leaning a bit further to capture her hand, I lift her from her seat, directing her towards the parking lot calmly, with my hand on the small of her back. I want this to be enjoyable and not stressful for her. "Yes, Precious. We have another surprise."

Run ahead; get us a room at the resort. Hurry, I instruct Dolos, trying not to snap at him. This isn't anyone's fault but ours, and we should have accounted for it.

As I continue to lead her through the rows of vehicles, her steps begin to falter, and she looks at me, beginning to panic. "Wh-what's going on? I feel…oh, God," she groans, her knees giving out. Before she can fall, I scoop her into my arms, carrying her the rest of the way to the resort, bridal-style.

Realization dawns across her features, her eyes trying to focus on the thoughts fleeting through her mind. "I-I'm going into heat," she says, more to herself than anything. Her overwhelming need floods our bond, and I really didn't want to have to walk into this hotel lobby with a raging hard-on, but it looks like that's exactly what's going to happen.

She's wriggling and whimpering in my arms, pulling on the buttons of my shirt. "Eris, please," she cries, and the pained sound of her voice nearly makes my knees buckle as I move faster. When we're almost to the sliding doors of the resort, I see Dolos dart in front of the door. *Got our room. Let's go,* he puffs, also struggling to keep his shit together.

"We're almost there, Precious. I promise we'll take care of you in just a minute," I pant, thankful the elevator and hallway were mostly empty.

A tear falls down her cheek, cracking my chest wide open. *Dolos, she's crying.* His wild eyes meet mine as we rush the remaining distance to our room.

Need. I'm enveloped in an all-consuming need like I've never known. My body is on fire. "Please," I whimper, more tears escaping my eyes.

Eris' eyes are burning and worrisome as he holds me close, promising to help soon. Dolos' eyes are wild as we continue down the hall.

We finally arrive at the door of a room within the resort and Dolos fumbles with the key card before bursting through the narrow doorway.

Eris moves to set me on the bed, but I latch onto him. "Please! It hurts!" I cry as another wave of burning desire crashes through me.

They're both frantic, and if I had any control over myself, I would feel terrible for worrying them like this. But I don't. I genuinely need them so badly it's starting to hurt, and I have no control over myself anymore.

Eris gently hands me to Dolos. "Give me just a minute, Precious. We'll make you feel better," he vows, ripping his clothes from his body the second I'm safely in Dolos' arms.

Once free of his own clothes, they work together to remove mine, kissing me, pinching my nipples, nipping at my skin, massaging my clit. It feels amazing, but it's barely taking the edge off the need rising within me.

The second I'm bare, I push Eris down on the bed and mount him. Reaching behind me, taking his hard length in my hand, I run it through my wet folds, lubricating him before aligning him with my entrance and impaling myself on him. While I release a cry of relief, he groans at my quick movements. Allowing myself a moment of circling my hips, I start riding him.

Dolos is swearing something under his breath and hastily removing his own clothes as I reach for him, my arm outstretched, needing him just as much as I need Eris. "Please, hurry…I need you," I pant as I continue to slam myself onto Eris to the hilt, my feverish need still only barely affected by my movements, still needing Dolos.

As if hearing my silent plea, he gathers my attention by trailing his fingers up my spine, wrapping my hair around his hand, and lightly tugging. "I'm gonna move you around a bit, okay?" he asks, eyes locked on mine as if he's trying to get to me through the fog of the lust overwhelming me. All I can do is nod.

He steps in between Eris' legs hanging over the side of the bed, places his hands on my thighs, and lifts me off his twin completely. A whimper escapes me at the loss, the ache mounting to unbearable levels. He moves me so that the tip of Eris' glistening shaft is now positioned at my rear entrance. Eris holds himself steady as I work his head through my tight ring of muscles, holding my breath.

Releasing a long breath when I've worked him all the way inside of me and settled on his lap, I begin to rock myself, his hard cock dragging along my every muscle. When it's so intense I feel as though I can barely breathe, Dolos chooses that instant to slam into me. A ragged cry of pleasure leaves me as they both groan.

He grips my hips hard, holding me down on top of Eris, unable to move as he commences pounding into me. My entire body is reeling with the intoxicating pleasure coursing through my veins and the erotic sounds coming from our bodies.

"Harder," I beg, and his hips take on a frantic pace. My arms are no longer able to hold me up, and I fall onto Eris, his arms immediately wrapping around me, one roughly grabbing and pinching my nipple, the other reaching lower.

When his fingers meet my swollen and sensitive clit, I gasp, somehow moaning louder when he focuses on my bundle of nerves, massaging it in a perfectly brutal rhythm, matching his brother's thrusts.

"Need you to come, Darling," Dolos orders through clenched teeth. I'm so fucking close, my eyes are crossing, my back arching harder, my body beginning to tremor until it detonates. Shockwaves of electric hot ecstasy shooting through my blood.

He thrusts two more times before he spears me with his knot, his hot cum coating my insides, and I scream another orgasm as his knot begins to stretch me euphorically.

The second I would normally be satiated and limp against them, the burning fire of my heat begins to rise once more. "Oh, Goddess," I cry, tears returning to my eyes. "It's…I need…please." I can't even explain to them what I need.

Eris is apparently able to translate my jumbled thoughts, which I'm sure are nonsensically filling our bond. "Again, Dolos," is all the notice he gives before he plants his spread feet on the edge of the bed somewhere and starts rutting into my ass from beneath me as I bellow into the air around us.

Dolos hisses, his swollen knot still lodged inside me with no signs of releasing him for another round. He grits his teeth and matches his twin's pace, unable to pull out of me, but driving his thick length and knot further inside of me, hitting that place inside of me that makes me scream.

My body is not my own. It's theirs. I'm going through some kind of blissed-out, out-of-body experience as they bring me closer to yet another orgasm. This one starts at the base of my spine as a heady fog spreads through my body, slowly rolling through my limbs, and I'm reeling, my head thrashing against Eris' chest.

From behind me, he bites hard on my mate mark as he shoves his knot through my tight ring of muscle, propelling me into a never-ending climax that twitches and burns through my core, a garbled shriek bursting from my lungs.

Chest heaving, lungs burning, I fall limp on top of him, and they both still. My hair and body are plastered to Eris as he coos and whispers against the shell of my ear, "My precious redemption. Our perfect mate with a fucking precious pussy."

My body shivers at his words, and even as spent as I am, just as the swelling of Dolos' knot wanes and he's able to remove himself from me, our mixed fluids dripping out of me, the heat begins to rise again.

Dolos steps away from me and returns almost immediately, sitting me up and impaling me further on Eris' still swollen cock. My head falls back on a moan, Dolos lifting my head again to get my attention, lifting a bottle to my mouth. "Drink some water, Darling. It looks like we're in for a long night," he says in that calm, loving way only he can, Eris chuckling beneath me.

By the time I drink the bottle dry, and he's given Eris one of his own, we're all hydrated just in time for the lust to haze all my senses once more.

Eris pulls out of me, laying me in the center of the bed, where they work my body together and in turns, for the next thirty-six hours before my heat finally dissipates and allows me to fall into a deep sleep.

32
DOLOS

When Runa's body finally falls into unconsciousness, Eris and I drop onto either side of her on the large bed. I only allow myself to lie there for a minute before getting up to get warm washcloths to clean her up.

Once she's all cleaned, I tuck in beside her, and we follow her into sleep.

🐾🐾

Waking first, an undetermined amount of time later, I find the dark sky outside beginning to lighten with the sun rising on a new day. Lifting myself from the bed, I take a look at my phone and realize we need to catch a flight home today if we want to get there in time for our Alpha and Luna's return.

Stretching my arms over my head, I move to clean up the mess we made of the room through her heat. After I'm satisfied with the state of our room, I place a room service order for everything on the breakfast menu, with extra pineapple, before moving back to the bed to wake Runa and Eris.

Runa's sleep-heavy eyes flutter open, tired but clear of the heat-induced glaze they had taken on. "Hi." She smiles, reaching for me.

"Hey, Darling. How are you feeling?" I ask her quietly, watching as she takes mental inventory of herself before her body answers for her, her growling stomach filling the room. She giggles before the knock at the door has her eyes narrowing on the sound. Laughing as I head towards the door, "Room service," I toss at her over my shoulder, a beautiful blush blooming on her cheeks.

When I return to the room with a cart full of food, making Runa's eyes damn near bug out of her head, I'm the only one with a scrap of clothing on as we dish out the food and enjoy a lazy breakfast together.

You get to tell her we have to go home today. I don't want to be the bad guy. I tell Eris through our bond, his forehead creasing.

"Precious?" he begins. Her wide eyes meet his, shrouded in hesitance at his tone. "We have to go home today, but we promise to bring you back soon."

Her eyes flash briefly with sadness before she shakes it away. "Maybe next time, we can all come?" she suggests sweetly.

The thought of all of us here together, her and Leera lying on the beach, sipping drinks and laughing while the guys try to learn how to surf, sounds perfect.

Once we've showered together and put ourselves back together in the other night's clothes, we hurry back to the vacation home to get all of our things.

With the car packed and idling in front of the house, Runa stands, taking it all in one more time before she nods and climbs into the car.

She's wearing her turquoise bracelet, her fingers tracing the shoreline through the window as our plane lifts above the island, her eyes full of love for this place.

After rummaging through our bags, I return to the cabin of the plane, plopping down beside her. *Ready, brother?* He nods.

"Remember when Dolos went missing for a bit?" he asks as he runs his fingers over her cheek.

She blushes furiously and nods, remembering them torturing me.

"Well, while the two of you tortured me," I say with mock offense, "I was at a local jeweler who specialized in custom works," I continue as her eyes widen, blushing again.

"We wanted you to have something special from us, from the island," he continues as I pull out the necklace we had made.

She gasps, her eyes filling with tears, her fingers tracing the design. Two waves coming together—one angry, one calm. Three sea turtles, all made with turquoise inlaid to match her bracelet. "It's perfect," she whispers, her voice watery with her unshed tears.

"You're perfect," my twin and I say in unison as I help her put on her necklace and we settle in for the long flight back to our family.

to be continued...

Acknowledgments

I so hope you all enjoyed Eris, Dolos, and Runa finally coming together. Since you all read My Pucking Mate, so many of you have made it very clear that you wanted the twins to have one mate. I had toyed with the ideas but never fully decided until you made sure I heard you all.

This is definitely different from the other novels, as we don't have the evolution of the main plot, no massive plot twists or gasping moments, but I hope the twin smut met your every expectation.

I can't believe I just finished writing my FOURTH book! I have so much in store for this amazing group and can't wait to continue to share it all with you and so many ideas for the future.

Thank Yous

My husband, for supporting me and being the perfect book husband, but if you could stop reading smut over my shoulder and making me blush profusely, that would be great.

My soul sister, for constantly making me feel like a best-selling author and promising to never let me lose touch.

My street team. Seriously. You guys. I could not do ANY OF THIS without you ALL!! Your support for me and my stories continues to overwhelm me in all the best ways.

Sarah, you've become such a good friend, and I love our chats. I can't wait for the surprises we have in store for our readers.

Aurelia for being able to read my mind and create the most stunning completed works of my books.

M.E. Kelley @TwistedAndTriggered—Thank you again for taking my scraps and turning them into a real blurb for the world to read.

Bedpost Books, for being my little author home for release parties. For your friendship. For the shirts you won't let me pay for. For loving Roman and Leera.

To all the little indie bookstores that have my books in your shop, it means the world to me that I can be a part of your story, and you mine.

My BETA readers! Mari, Karlee, Carrie, D, and Mars!

To you. My reader. I'll never know what I did to deserve your love for me and my world, but I whole-heartedly promise to treasure that love forever.

Thank you again to all my feral babes who help make the NSFW art happen: Katie Riley, Marissa Renteria, Eva G, Sarah Cloud, Maleny Roman-Ruiz, Erin Cooper, Crystal Doneghy, Amina Gorlacheva, Samantha Mackey, and Leslie King!

About The Author

Izzy Elliott is a Midwest mom of four, married to her very own soulmate. In the real world, she works full-time for your run-of-the-mill, corporate nine-to-five. When she's not working or chasing kids, she's reading, writing, traveling, or shopping.

Follow Along

Instagram as @IzzyElliottWrites, where you can find all my main links to things like Beventi for signing event preorders, VIP Facebook Group, current ARC and PR Box Applications, Newsletter sign-up, and even a Discord (that I'm not very good at remembering to use).

TikTok under IzzyElliottWrites

Facebook as Izzy Elliott

Want to know what I'm reading? Follow my Bookstagram account @ WhereIzzyReads

Visit izzyelliott.com for signed books, book boxes, merch, and more!

www.ingramcontent.com/pod-product-compliance
Lightning Source LLC
Chambersburg PA
CBHW030337310726
48979CB00001B/76